TURQUOISE DECEPTION

TURQUOISE DECEPTION

A Paradox Murder Mystery

Book Two

Charles J Thayer

TURQUOISE DECEPTION

*Twenty years from now you will be more
disappointed by the things you didn't do
than by the things you did do.*

*So throw off the bowlines.
Sail away from the safe harbor.
Catch the trade winds in your sails.*

Explore. Dream. Discover.

Mark Twain

Prologue

My name is Steve Wilson. A year ago I was senior auditor for one of our nation's largest banks in New York City. My specialties were fraud, money laundering and cybersecurity investigations.

After thirty-five years as an auditor I was ready to start a new chapter in my life and took advantage of an unexpected early retirement package at age fifty-five. My only retirement plan consisted of traveling to Maine to write a murder mystery - in other words, I really had no plan.

My years of unraveling financial mysteries from the safety of my bank office did not prepare me for the dangers I faced in Maine when my curiosity about a dead lobsterman and three missing photos almost got me killed. Death Trap, my first book, describes last year's unexpected adventure.

Maybe it's just a coincidence, but this adventure also starts with a dead body.

Steve

1

3rd Week of January

"His body was discovered shortly after sunrise in Thunderball Grotto, an underwater cave near Staniel Cay in The Bahamas. The Bahamian authorities called it an accidental drowning. Let me explain the problem."

I was being briefed by Mark Bouchard, head of the financial crimes unit for the FBI, at his office in New York. Mark has been my primary contact at the FBI for the past fifteen years and we have developed a strong professional relationship.

"The dead man's name is Keith Jones. He was manager of a branch office in Rockland for a bank headquartered in Portland, Maine. He told both his boss and his wife he was going to Fort Lauderdale to attend a banking conference being held in early November. However, he deceived both of them and he did not attend that conference. No one knew he was going to The Bahamas. It took time to even confirm his identity as he was only wearing swimming shorts and there was no identification on the body."

"Jones paid cash for a three-day stay in a cottage at a small resort called the Staniel Cay Yacht Club. Rumor has it that he was with a woman at the Yacht Club but, if true, her identity and whereabouts are unknown."

"After his death, his wife discovered $5,000 in cash in his desk at home with a key to an unknown safe deposit box at another bank. Their family attorney discovered another $50,000 in cash in that safe deposit box as he took steps to settle the estate."

"As you would expect, the bank has audited of all his accounts to determine if any of this mystery cash resulted from an embezzlement. The bank's initial audit reports indicate all the bank's accounts are in balance and no funds appear to be missing. As a result, the source of this cash is still a puzzle."

"You will recall when we had dinner together last month, I mentioned that Amanda was involved in a situation where I thought you could be helpful. In fact, she is a family friend of the bank's President and he asked her for advice."

"As we have discussed, I think your experience and knowledge makes you a unique resource for community banks across our country. Helping this bank determine the source of this mystery cash could be an excellent way for you to start a private consulting practice, should you decide to do so."

"James Parker, the bank's President is expecting your call."

#   #   #

I had just finished the working draft of Death Trap, my new book describing my near death adventure in Maine this past year. I now had time for a break and helping this bank sounded interesting. Mark's suggestion I help smaller banks solve fraud investigations was an intriguing idea.

Mark didn't elaborate about Amanda's involvement but I looked forward to seeing her again. Amanda Smith was the investigator with the sheriff's department who solved the murders in Stone Harbor last year.

I called James Parker and we arranged to meet in Portland the following Monday.

2

4th Week of January

On Monday morning I did a short workout at my nearby gym. I stand a little over six feet tall and regular exercise helps keep my weight under two hundred pounds. I returned to my co-op apartment to shower and pack for my trip. While shaving I noticed my dark hair was showing signs of gray.

I selected a solid gray winter-weight suit to wear with a blue dress shirt and plain tie. I want to look the part of a conservative bank auditor when discussing a new financial problem. Fortunately, having lived in New York for fifteen years, I also have a very warm overcoat, gloves and a hat for freezing weather. To be prepared, I packed my suitcase with another winter suit and sufficient dress shirts for a week of work in Maine. I had no idea what to expect on my first consulting assignment.

Parker told me he would arrange for someone to meet my afternoon flight and drive me to the bank's headquarters in downtown Portland. As I looked across the airport lobby for my contact, I spotted a tall blonde with a familiar face and to my surprise it was Amanda! It was below freezing and she was in a bright red ski jacket and, as always, her long blonde hair was in a ponytail. She was wearing black leather boots with her trademark blue jeans and carrying a small black leather backpack.

"Amanda, great to see you. I was expecting someone from the bank."

"We thought it might be better if I drove you to the bank and introduced you. James is an old family friend, and I encouraged him to talk to you about this unexplained cash. He was very proud of Keith Jones and planned to promote him this year. James is really upset, and he wants this puzzle solved. He can't understand what happened."

Amanda introduced me to Parker when we arrived at the bank's headquarters. He closed the door to his private office and motioned toward two chairs and couch next to a small coffee table; "Please make yourselves comfortable".

Parker looked the part of a bank president; silver-gray hair, dark blue pinstripe suit with matching vest, average height, fairly stocky and in his early sixties. He started our meeting with some questions;

"Mr. Wilson, please tell me, how do you think you can help us? I was surprised you would even consider working with a smaller bank like ours given your background in New York."

I responded; "Please call me Steve. I am not certain how I can help. I always enjoy solving financial crimes but I need to learn more about your financial systems and controls before I can answer your question."

Parker replied; "Understood and please call me James. Amanda told me you were retired but you don't look retirement age - what's the story?"

"I started working at a small community bank in Kentucky when I was in college. Following twenty years of bank mergers, I was senior auditor of the bank headquartered in New York City."

"I suspect everyone was surprised when, after thirty-five years, I accepted the early retirement package the bank announced for long-term employees last year. The bank's President thought I was just having a mid-life crisis and would change my mind but I was ready to start a new chapter in my life."

"As you know; technology, competition and constantly changing regulations have all made banking more complex. One thing has remained constant; people try to game the system. I always get great satisfaction when I can identify and solve a financial puzzle. I look forward to helping you solve this mystery."

James then invited the bank's young auditor, Tory Forbes, to join us and we all moved to the small conference table in the corner of his office.

Tory reported; "Keith Jones was a regional branch manager based in Rockland with additional responsibility for branch offices in Camden and Belfast. My investigation included all his customer relationships at all three branch office locations."

"My review of Keith's personal and customer accounts at each location uncovered no suspicious transactions in his personal accounts. His large customers have all verified the transactions and balances in their accounts. As a result, the bank's financial records and accounts appear to be in order. I am frustrated and have not identified the source of this mysterious cash."

James arranged for Tory to drive me to Rockland the following morning so we could both examine everything at the bank's branch office again firsthand.

#   #   #

Amanda then drove me to my hotel, and she suggested a restaurant for us to have dinner. Amanda waited in the hotel lobby while I checked in and dropped my bag in my room.

Amanda Smith is a crime investigator with a county sheriff's office in Downeast Maine. She is not required to wear a traditional police uniform and she almost always wears blue jeans with colorful sweaters and carries a small backpack.

We became acquainted when she was assigned to investigate a suspected murder that occurred during my stay in Stone Harbor. I had learned during her investigation that this tall, physically fit, attractive young woman with a blonde ponytail that looked and dressed like a college student was actually about forty. I enjoyed helping Amanda with her investigation last year and was surprised she was in Portland as it was out of her official territory.

Amanda had selected a quiet downtown restaurant where we could talk and, after we were seated, she made a surprise announcement.

"Mark wanted to let me tell you the news. I joined his financial crimes team at the FBI on January 1st. I am based in Portland and will work for Mark on assignments across the county."

I was speechless for a moment then said;

"Amanda, Mark never even hinted that this was in the works. It's an amazing opportunity for you to work with his team - they are first rate. How did this happen?"

"The FBI posted an opening several months ago and I submitted my application. I applied with the FBI when I graduated from law school in Boston. However, no openings existed in their Portland office at that time and I wanted to move back to Maine. When this opening occurred I decided, after fifteen years with the sheriff's office, it was time for me to reach out to the FBI."

"My undergraduate degree is in accounting and business. My undergraduate and law degrees combined with my experience as an investigator fit the profile that qualified me for my interview with Mark in New York last October."

"That interview was shortly after I was assigned to investigate the potential murder in Stone Harbor and met you. Mark recognized the coincidence and your evaluation of my work is probably the reason I got this job. So, dinner is on me tonight."

I asked; "You now live in Portland? Are you working on this bank issue? Do you still get to wear blue jeans?"

She cut me off; "Slow down, we have time to talk. Yes, I have moved to Portland. No, I am not working on the bank issue - the bank hasn't reported a crime for me to investigate. And, yes, depending on the assignment I can still wear my blue jeans."

Amanda continued; "I am truly excited by this opportunity. As you know, Mark runs a specialized unit to investigate financial crimes with FBI agents in offices around the country. We don't have designated territories and Mark assigns all investigations to designated team members. He expects all of us to work together as needed and he prefers a less formal atmosphere. He wants his team to use first names, not titles, and he encouraged me to call him Mark. It will take me time to adjust as the county sheriff's office had a more formal structure."

We enjoyed an excellent lobster dinner and pleasant evening together. As we arrived back at my hotel, I said; "Amanda, it's great to see you again. Thanks for the news - congratulations."

"Thank you. I always enjoy visiting with you."

3

Tory picked me up at my hotel at daybreak on Tuesday morning and she drove us to the bank's branch in Rockland. Tory was just over five feet tall and was wearing a long dark blue winter coat with a stocking cap and brown leather boots. Dressing for freezing weather was the uniform of the day for everyone I was to meet at the bank. Once inside the bank I noticed her conservative soft blue pantsuit complimented her short light brown hairstyle.

Our two-hour drive gave us time to talk. I learned Tory had an accounting degree from a university in Maine and had worked as an auditor at the bank for the past four years. She was recently married to a college classmate who worked for a local CPA firm. I was impressed with her dedication to doing a professional job for the bank.

This was my first experience working with a community bank and I was concerned Tory would consider my presence an intrusion and resent my involvement.

I asked; "Tory, what would you like to know about me and why I was asked to help you with your investigation."

Tory replied; "Mr. Wilson, Mr. Parker is concerned about what has happened. We all liked Keith Jones, and he was considered a rising star at the bank. We all knew he was ambitious, but he was an excellent manager. As you will discover, he was respected by his staff. We are all very confused by what happened."

"The staff knows he didn't attend that banking conference when he was found dead in The Bahamas. My investigation has started rumors, but we have made no announcements about the unexplained cash we have located. I welcome all the help I can get to solve this puzzle."

"Tory, please call me Steve. I sincerely appreciate your attitude. I thought you might resent my intrusion."

Tory responded; "I already knew a little about you before Mr. Parker told me you were coming up to meet with us. I attended a couple of conferences for bank auditors where you made presentations. I look forward to your help and welcome any career advice you may have for me."

"Tory, few college graduates recognize how valuable an early auditing assignment will be to their future careers in banking. As an auditor you have the opportunity to learn about and evaluate every aspect of bank operations. You will gain a broad understanding of banking, whereas, other college recruits generally only learn a specific function such as lending or branch operations."

"In my case, I elected to remain in audit after college and became a specialist in investigating financial crimes. Many of my colleagues have used their audit experience as a stepping stone to more specialized jobs. Their broad understanding of banking helped several of them advance to very senior management positions."

Tory directed me to the conference room she was utilizing for her investigation when we arrived at the branch office. She removed her laptop from her computer bag and logged into the bank's computer system. We systematically reviewed the work she had already undertaken. She was correct, all the accounts appeared to be in order.

We took a break for lunch and walked to a nearby restaurant. Once we were seated, I asked;

"Tory, if you were going to embezzle funds from the bank wouldn't you cover your tracks and make certain everything in both your personal accounts and your customer accounts appeared to be in order and nothing was missing?"

She responded; "Of course I would."

I coached; "Then we need to look for his tracks - we need to think like a criminal. How could he embezzle over fifty thousand dollars and keep the accounts in balance?"

When we returned to the branch, Tory logged my laptop computer into the bank's system with read-only access. Together we reviewed large deposit accounts and, as we were about to finish, Tory said; "I had to do extra analysis on two customers with multiple accounts."

"The first account is this auto dealership that had an unusual number of regular cash deposits."

After we reviewed the account, I said; "Tory, nice work. I consider this type of activity to be a sign of possible money laundering. I suggested you do additional analysis on these cash transactions."

"Steve, I was surprised to find these two accounts with multi-million dollar transactions at the branch. However, the Portland law firm that established the accounts verified all the transactions."

"Interesting, I'm also curious. I suggest you ask the law firm why these large accounts were opened at the Rockland branch rather than at the bank's main office in Portland."

Tory had arranged two rooms for our overnight stay at a nearby motel used by traveling bank employees. She said she was tired and would order room service. I had visited Rockland during my visit to Maine last year and walked a few blocks to the main street to eat dinner at a local restaurant. I wished we had extra time so I could again visit the Wyeth art exhibits.

I used the treadmill in the motel's small workout room before showering in the morning. It's not always easy in the winter weather, but I try to walk or workout almost every morning.

On Wednesday morning, we shifted our attention to the large customer loans that Jones had managed. Tory had already worked with the bank's credit department to confirm all the customer information and loan balances were in order. Tory was doing a professional job.

Tory then shifted our focus; "Steve, as a regional manager, Jones's lending authority permitted him to make loans up to $100,000 without additional credit approval and oversight. He was primarily responsible for all customer information and loan monitoring. The credit department will only get involved if the customer's loan payments are not made in a timely manner. I have confirmed that all the loan documentation and payments are up-to-date on each of these loans."

As we reviewed the files, I noticed that a number of the bank's customers managed all their deposit and loan accounts online with only limited information mailed to the customers.

I asked; "I think a post office box is the only address for these accounts. Is that correct?"

"Yes."

"If that's the case, then I suggest you compare the customer information Keith entered into the bank's computer system with public records to confirm accuracy."

Everything matched until; "Steve, come look at this. This firm is not registered to do business in Maine and the street address appears to be an empty lot."

Tory's laptop was open to her satellite map program and I could see the address marker was over an empty lot. I replied; "Well done. You check the rest of those accounts and I will examine the transactions in this account."

It didn't take long for me to review the loan and checking accounts established for this customer as only a few transactions had occurred in the past three years. I briefed Tory on my findings.

"Keith approved a loan of $75,000 for this account

about three years ago. The loan matures next month and it only required quarterly interest payments. Everything in the loan's documentation has been entered correctly, the interest rate is consistent with bank policy and all payments have been made on time. This loan would not have triggered a credit department review."

"The loan proceeds were deposited into a newly established checking account and $70,000 was sent by wire transfer to an account at a bank in Boston within a few days. Then, wire transfers were made back to this checking account from that account in Boston to pay any interest due on a timely basis. Those are the only transactions."

"The signatures on the new account files show both the loan and checking accounts were opened by a Kenneth Johnson. Keith scanned no form of identification into the bank's systems."

Tory then reported; "Steve, I have found a second loan for $50,000 made four years ago with a different customer name but with the same post office box and empty lot address."

A short while later we confirmed the same pattern of transactions and account information for the second account.

The two loan accounts had different company names but listed the same empty lot address with the same post office box address, phone number and email information.

Tory placed her cell phone on speaker and dialed the number listed for both accounts. After a few rings the call went to voice mail and a message;

"Thank you for calling. Sorry, we are unable to answer your call at this time but we will return it as promptly as possible. Please leave a message."

Tory's face turned pale, and she said; "Steve, I am certain that is Keith's voice."

Tory had uncovered the two suspicious accounts, but we still had more homework to do. We stayed overnight in Rockland again so we could conclude our investigation the next day. On our drive back to the motel we confirmed the address listed for both accounts was in fact an empty lot owned by the adjoining business that a small sign showed they used for extra parking.

4

We returned to the Rockland branch on Thursday morning to diagram the transactions. We confirmed the loan proceeds from both accounts had been wired to the same account at a bank in Boston. The funds to make interest payments on the fictitious loans were wired back to the bank from the same account in Boston.

Tory emailed a balance request to the bank in Boston and we were shocked when the bank confirmed a current account balance of $65,000. The bank also confirmed it was an online small business account established by Keith Jones. The bank provided Tory with a scan of the driver's license Keith used to open the account.

Once we completed the diagram of accounts and transactions, we were faced with a puzzling question. We had established that Jones had made loans to fictitious firms that totaled $125,000 and that $115,000 had been transferred to the account at the bank in Boston. Almost $22,000 had been withdrawn from the account in Boston to pay the interest due on both fictitious loans over the past four years.

The fictitious deposit accounts at the Rockland branch each had a remaining balance of $5,000. So, the combined cash balances remaining in all three fictitious bank accounts totaled $75,000.

When we added the $75,000 on deposit at the two banks to the $55,000 in suspicious cash located by Jones's wife and their family attorney, we had a total of $130,000.

The remaining cash of $130,000 exceeded the total loan proceeds of $125,000 Jones had embezzled. It now appeared no money was missing and the bank would have a full recovery!

We still had a mystery. What was the source of the extra cash? Why did Jones embezzle and pay interest on fictitious loans if he didn't need the money? Tory would need to do some additional investigation.

I was impressed, Tory had identified the fictitious accounts and the embezzlement. This was her first fraud investigation, but I suspected it would not be her last. I was confident the bank had a good auditor.

We drove back to Portland that afternoon and Tory reported her findings to James Parker.

# # #

Parker had arranged a meeting with Keith Jones's wife, Mary, for Friday afternoon. There was no evidence she was involved in her husband's embezzlement and, based on Tory's analysis, the bank would suffer no loss. However, we all wanted to see if she could add any additional information to our investigation.

Mary arrived in the early afternoon with her family attorney to meet with Tory and myself. This was an awkward meeting as Mary was obviously very upset by her husband's deceptive actions and his unexplained death in The Bahamas.

We closed the door to a private conference room and made it clear to her that she was not being accused of anything. We offered our sympathy for her situation.

I then opened our discussion; "Mary, I am sorry to say, we have evidence Keith embezzled the cash you discovered at home and in the safe deposit box discovered by your attorney. We thank you for reporting this money and delivering it to the bank for safekeeping until the source of the funds could be identified."

"We have also identified other funds and to our surprise we might have uncovered more money than Keith embezzled."

"Mary, is there anything you can tell us about the source of this cash and help everyone understand what has happened?"

Mary replied; "No, I don't know how he got that money. I am still in shock and am glad my family and friends are being so supportive. I had no idea Keith was going to The Bahamas. I didn't even know he had a passport. I don't have one and we never traveled out of the country, not even to Canada."

"I was surprised when his passport was returned when his body was finally sent back to Maine. I brought it today for you to see."

Mary handed me Keith's passport and a quick review indicated official entries from The Bahamas for four visits in the past two years.

"Mary, this indicates Keith made at least four visits to The Bahamas in the past couple of years. I see stamps for three visits to Nassau and the most recent one to Staniel Cay. What excuse did he give you for his being away from home?"

"On two other occasions he told me he was attending a banking conference in Florida, just like this time. Keith also made occasional overnight business trips to visit customers in Boston. Keith was very ambitious and he wanted to impress Mr. Parker with his ability to generate new business."

"Do you have any idea why Keith would have started to embezzle money about four years ago? Did you have some financial problems?"

"Not that I knew about. I also work and we always seemed to have enough money. We purchased our house in Rockland about five years ago and I understood we had an excellent credit score."

After a pause; "Keith did like to gamble and about that time he would visit the casinos on weekends. He seemed really frustrated several years ago, and he stopped going as frequently. He never told me he had any big losses but I must admit I was pretty worried for a time. I was very relieved when he started telling me he had a good night."

"Mr. Wilson, the rumors suggest Keith was with another woman, is that true?"

"Mary, I don't know if he was or not. We don't know why Keith was in The Bahamas and our internal audit will be completed if the bank has a full recovery of the funds Keith embezzled. No legal action will be necessary if, as we currently believe, Keith acted alone."

"Is there anything else you think might be helpful in understanding what has happened?"

"No, I am hurt and embarrassed. Keith deceived me about going to The Bahamas and this money. I don't know why he did it. I thought we were happy."

At that point Mary lost her composure. We left her alone to be consoled by her attorney who was apparently a close family friend.

#   #   #

That evening it was my turn to take Amanda to dinner and bring her up-to-date.

"Amanda, Tory has uncovered an embezzlement. However, I see no reason to open an official investigation by the FBI as Jones is dead, no money appears to be missing and everything indicates he acted alone. Tory is preparing reports for the bank's regulators."

"However, we have lots of unanswered questions. Why did Jones embezzle the money? Did he have large gambling losses? Why is there a small surplus of cash? Did his gambling luck change? Why was he in The Bahamas? Were the trips to The Bahamas business or pleasure?"

Jones was dead and unable to answer any of our questions.

5

1st Week of February

Mark was right, I enjoyed my consulting assignment and helping Tory uncover the Jones embezzlement. Parker was pleased, and he asked me to provide the bank with guidance on overall risk management. It was time for me to formalize my new business.

Picking a name for my new financial consulting firm was a significant challenge. Over the years I had observed many financial crimes are structured as a paradox to confuse and misdirect any investigation.

The Cambridge Dictionary defines a paradox as; *"a situation or statement that seems impossible or is difficult to understand because it contains two opposite facts or characteristics."*

The most recent example of such a paradox was the Jones embezzlement - [1] Jones embezzled the money but [2] no money was missing.

After thinking about a few other names, I selected Paradox Research as the name for my new firm and printed a few business cards.

Steve Wilson
Paradox Research
www.Paradox-Research.com
Paradox09A@Gmail.com

Selecting an email address was equally frustrating. I wanted to use the name of my new firm but securing that email address required some additional symbols. After doing a little research I added 09A [zero-nine-A] the uniform crime code for murder. That just seemed fitting after my unexpected adventure in Maine last year.

When I shared my new business card with Mark he smiled and commented; "Not certain I want to ask why you added 09A to your email address. I hope it's not a prediction of future events."

\#   \#   \#

The balance of my week was devoted to discussing Death Trap with Wanda, the independent book editor I had retained. My original retirement plan was to write a series of fictitious murder mysteries based on my prior criminal investigations at the bank. However, I changed direction and wrote Death Trap based on last year's events in Maine.

Wanda is a college English professor, and we were meeting in a small conference room at the school.

When I arrived; "Steve, thank you for coming over today. I appreciate having the opportunity to work with you. I enjoyed reading your draft of Death Trap and, if it's OK, I want to ask you a few questions before we review my notes."

"First, I'm always curious why someone writes a book - writing anything for publication is always a challenge."

"Wanda, I didn't have a plan when I retired and I need intellectual activity to keep my mind active. I read murder mysteries on late night flights. I call them 'airplane books' and writing my own murder mystery seemed like fun."

"Why did you write your novel in the first person?"

"Death Trap is based on my notes describing the events in my daily calendar. I want my readers to feel like they are having a personal conversation with me about those events."

"Steve, if Death Trap is based on your actual experiences in Maine last year - then why did you decide to write your story as fiction?"

"Many of the events were disturbing to the residents of these small coastal towns. I made friends with these people so I thought it would be best to disguise their names and some locations."

"I'm curious why you have used the page format typically used by professional business publications rather than the style generally used for fiction?"

I responded; "My experience is writing business reports and articles for professional publications. I prefer this easy-to-read format."

"Steve, I seldom see photos in a work of fiction - why did you include your photos?"

"My photos add to the non-fiction feel of the book - wouldn't you share photos with me if you were telling me your story?"

Wanda replied; "Yes, you are right, I enjoy sharing photos with my friends. I find your photos and the description of your day on a lobster boat to be helpful and educational."

"Thank you, I want my books to be both educational and entertaining."

The balance of our session was devoted to Wanda's edits to my text and clarification of events in the story. I was eager to print a few proof copies and get pre-publication feedback from friends.

6

2nd Week of February

I wanted to avoid the distractions of New York City when I started my novel. So last summer, based on a recommendation from friends, I selected Stone Harbor Inn in Maine as my temporary home to focus on my writing.

Anne Baxter owned and managed the Inn and, although we had a rocky beginning, we found ourselves in a personal relationship. Stone Harbor Inn is closed for the winter and, as planned, Anne is now visiting with her friends, Ken and Frances Stewart, in Fort Lauderdale.

Anne is dedicated to the management of her Inn and during my stay at her Inn our relationship was more businesslike than personal. On the other hand, I discovered Anne relaxed and could be very affectionate when away from the Inn. We enjoyed being together in New York during December and made plans to meet again in Florida.

My flight arrived at Fort Lauderdale International on Sunday afternoon and, as I walked through security, I spotted Anne in a yellow sundress that highlighted her pulled-back brunette hairstyle. Anne has a talent for matching her hairstyle and wardrobe to fit her statuesque figure. She always looks sophisticated in any situation; working at her Inn, navigating her boat, walking down 5th Avenue or meeting me at the airport.

After a warm greeting, I picked up my bag from the luggage belt and Anne drove us north on US1 to Las Olas Boulevard. We headed east on Las Olas passing several blocks of high-end shops and entered the Las Olas Isles.

Fort Lauderdale - Venice of America

This was my first visit to Fort Lauderdale's unique waterfront neighborhoods, known as the Venice of America, with their large impressive homes and yachts docked along private canals that parallel each street.

The Stewarts live in a classic two-story Mediterranean style home located near a charming cul-de-sac on one of the Las Olas Isles. Their home has a long dock for their yacht and a small guest house where Anne was staying.

We all shared cocktails in the main house that evening and I enjoyed getting to know the Stewarts. Ken was about my height of six feet, fit, suntanned with thinning gray hair and a friendly smile. Ken made me feel at ease as he described their background.

"Frances and I both enjoy cruising on our boat. We purchased our Fleming 55 six years before I sold my business in Illinois and retired five years ago. We kept our Fleming at Bahia Mar Marina and visited Fort Lauderdale as often as possible. We enjoy frequent cruises to Miami, Palm Beach or the nearby Bahamas. We like this area and when I retired we purchased our home on the Las Olas Isles so we could keep our boat on our own dock."

"We now have more time to enjoy cruising and for the past five years have spent several months in The Bahamas. We like Highbourne Cay in the Exumas and frequently utilize that island as our base of operations."

Frances politely interrupted; "Don't let Ken get started on cruising in The Bahamas! We need to learn a little more about you."

Frances is a very elegant woman. She was wearing a pale green fitted designer dress that complimented her short stature and slender figure. Her short silver-gray hair style accented her natural features and a relaxed friendly smile.

Frances added; "We need to share a little history before Ken sidetracks us with cruising adventures. Anne and I were roommates in college and we have remained friends for the past thirty years. Ken and I have visited Stone Harbor and we stayed with Anne at her Inn on several occasions. Anne has been gracious enough to show us the beautiful Maine coastline from her boat."

Frances then shifted the conversation; "So Steve, tell us how you and Anne got to know one another. Ken only knows you are a retired banker that stayed at her Inn last year."

Anne looked in my direction and waited for me to answer.

"Well, it's a complicated story. Anne may have told you I am just finishing a novel based on what happened in Stone Harbor last year. I will make certain you get an autographed copy."

"I was in banking for thirty-five years and took advantage of an early retirement package offered to long-term employees last year. When I retired I was a senior auditor of the bank in New York."

"My decision to retire was rather sudden and I had made no plans for my retirement. I have always liked to write so, with little planning, went to Maine last summer to write a murder mystery novel. I booked a room at the Stone Harbor Inn for six weeks to get away and start my book - that's when Anne and I first met."

I then gave a brief description of events related to the deserted lobster boat, the death of a lobsterman and my curiosity about three missing photos. They were shocked when Anne shared how close we both came to being killed.

Fortunately, Anne and I were able to laugh while describing the ups and downs of our relationship.

I found both Ken and Frances to be charming people. We adjourned outside to their pool deck to enjoyed the excellent shrimp and pasta dinner Frances had prepared. They shared a few stories with us about cruising in The Bahamas while we ate dinner. I was impressed the two of them were experienced and comfortable navigating their Fleming 55 without crew. Their boat was large enough to have two extra cabins for guests and they enjoyed frequent visits from family and friends. I accepted Ken's offer to tour their Fleming 55 the next morning.

After dinner, they left Anne and me alone to enjoy an evening together on the small private patio at the guest house. It was good to see Anne again but in some respects it felt like we were starting over. We have art, books, boating and other interests in common and we both seem to enjoy being together. We had frequent romantic moments during her stay with me in New York but we both remained very cautious about our relationship and neither of us voiced the 'love' commitment.

#   #   #

Fort Lauderdale calls itself the "Yachting Capital of the World" and on Tuesday afternoon Anne borrowed the Stewart's center console Boston Whaler to show me the yachts and houses along the Intracoastal Waterway. As we cruised along the waterways viewing impressive homes and yachts, I learned Anne was far more experienced than she had shared with me in Maine.

My family in Kentucky had always owned sailboats on the Kentucky Lakes. I joined a sailing club while living in Chicago and chartered sailboats a few times in the Chesapeake and Caribbean after moving to New York. I was comfortable sailing small cruising sailboats but Anne was far more experienced operating a powerboat.

The Miami International Boat Show takes place in mid-February and we decided it would be fun to attend. It's a sprawling event along the Miami waterfront with about 2,000 boats of every design and size on exhibit. Ken arranged for us to get special Premier Day tickets for opening day on Thursday. The overwhelming size of the show required us to carefully review the show program before walking the docks to locate all the boats we wanted to visit.

The more I looked at various designs displayed at the show the more I liked a Downeast lobster boat design like Anne's. No question, I was getting hooked as we talked to boat brokers and boarded selected boats at the show. Attending the show renewed my interest in finding a boat to buy.

On the drive back to Fort Lauderdale I told Anne I was serious about looking at Downeast lobster boat designs for sale. She was excited and volunteered to see what boats might be available in South Florida. Anne enjoyed the warm weather and sunshine but it was clear she had always worked and welcomed a new project to keep her busy.

The final weekend of my visit was spent visiting with a couple of boat brokers in Fort Lauderdale and looking at a few other designs that might also meet my expectations. I wanted something large enough to live and work on for periods of time but small enough to navigate alone. It was clear I needed to do some serious homework to avoid making a stupid, impulsive decision.

#   #   #

The Stewart's guest house was very comfortable. Anne and I enjoyed relaxing on the private patio, swimming in their pool and dining at some fabulous waterfront restaurants during our visit together in Fort Lauderdale. As time passed, we relaxed and again shared a few romantic moments.

7

3rd Week of February

I headed back to New York from Fort Lauderdale on Monday evening to exchange my Florida suitcase for appropriate Maine clothing. This was a less formal visit to the bank in Portland, so I packed my L.L.Bean clothing for freezing temperatures.

On Tuesday I had a meeting with Tory to review her findings on the potential auto dealer money laundering scheme. I was impressed with her work as she carefully presented her analysis of the auto dealer's bank accounts for my review.

"The auto dealer experienced a dramatic increase in cash sales of small used cars during the past year. Most of these cash sales were regular transactions with just one car buyer."

"Neither the bank nor the auto dealer is technically required to report these individual cash purchases as each sale is less than $10,000, the threshold for reporting suspicious transactions to federal regulators. As a result, all the transactions technically meet the bank's legal requirement."

Tory explained; "They appear to have a rather simple scheme to permit the used car buyer to turn cash into legitimate bank deposits. The buyer pays cash to the dealer to buy the car and the dealer then writes the buyer a check to repurchase the car. The timing of the transactions is suspicious and several of the auto registration documents indicate the same used car was sold back and forth between the auto dealer and the same car buyer."

"My investigation indicates the car buyer in this scheme owns a local restaurant with accounts at another bank. I suspect the restaurant owner is engaged in this activity to avoid reporting cash receipts as taxable income. The appropriate reports are filed with bank regulators and any future action is in the hands of law enforcement."

Tory also reported; "I asked the accountant at Alexander's law firm in Portland why he had established those large accounts with Keith Jones at the Rockland branch office. He told me Jones had attended college with Alexander's son and the accounts had been opened as a favor during a new account contest at the bank. In fact, these accounts have now been closed and transferred to another bank in Boston."

Finally, Tory also told me she had been working

with an auditor at the bank in Boston to analyze the account Jones used to transfer the funds related to his embezzlement. Tory had prepared a summary for me to review.

"I was able to confirm that Keith Jones used the same empty lot address, email and phone number at the bank in Boston that he used to establish the fictitious accounts at our bank. However, he had to use his own name to open that account in Boston."

"Steve, my summary shows we still have a major mystery. Monthly deposits of $4,000 each were made into that account in Boston for twelve months. The first six deposits were cash deposits made at a branch in Boston. The remainder of those unexplained deposits were wire transfers from a bank in The Bahamas."

"During the last six months the wire transfers from that bank in Nassau increased to $8,000 each month. I am trying to get more information on that account in The Bahamas. I have no idea how or why Keith obtained that additional $96,000."

I was impressed; "Tory, well done. That was great teamwork with the auditor in Boston."

"Thanks, Nancy and I went to college together, it was easy to work with her. We now know that when you add that $96,000 to the $115,000 transferred from our bank that a total of $211,000 was deposited into the account in Boston."

Keith Jones Embezzlement Summary				
Accounts - Rockland			**Checking Account - Boston**	
Rockland #1			**Deposits**	
Loan Amount	$50,000		Deposit Rockland #1	$45,000
To Checking Acct	$50,000		Deposit Rockland #2	$70,000
Sent to Boston	($45,000)		Total from Rockland	$115,000
Cash Balance	$5,000		*Cash Deposits?*	$24,000
			Wires - Bahamas?	$72,000
Rockland #2			*Unexplained Deposits*	*$96,000*
Loan Amount	$75,000		Total Deposits	$211,000
To Checking Acct	$75,000			
Sent to Boston	($70,000)		**Withdrawals**	
Cash Balance	$5,000		Interest on Loans	($22,000)
			Credit Cards?	($55,000)
Combined Accounts			Keith Jones - Cash?	($69,000)
Combined Loans	$125,000		Total Withdrawn	($146,000)
Sent to Boston	($115,000)		Cash Balance	$65,000
Combined Cash	$10,000			
Cash at House	$5,000		Keith Jones - Cash	$69,000
Safe Deposit Box	$50,000		House/Safety Box	($55,000)
Boston Account	$65,000		Jones Spent?	$14,000
Total Cash	$130,000			

"We also know Keith withdrew $22,000 to pay interest on the fictitious loans. Shortly after the account was opened, he wrote checks for $55,000 to pay credit card balances and, over the past two years, he withdrew another $69,000 in cash leaving the balance of $65,000."

She added; "I assume the $55,000 in cash discovered by Mary and their attorney was part of the $69,000 in cash he withdrew. He probably just spent the other $14,000."

"Tory, let's follow up on the gambling connection. Casinos accept credit cards so you might have identified the reason for his initial embezzlement."

I added; "You should be able to contact the banks that issued his credit cards and determine if any transactions occurred at casinos."

I was pleased Tory was quickly learning how to look 'behind the curtain' and identify suspicious transactions. She clearly understood that just having the paperwork in order was not the objective of an effective audit.

Tory was right, we still had a major mystery. What was the source of the $96,000 of unexplained deposits? Why was $72,000 wired to Keith Jones from a bank in The Bahamas?

8

I had a few extra days in Maine and rented a car to explore lobster boats for sale. Lobster boats are known for their seakeeping ability and classic appearance. Lobster boat designs now serve as cruisers, sport-fishers and workboats of all types around the world.

The temperature was below freezing and snow covered much of the state. As a result, boats were not in the water but I could arrange with brokers to see a few boats in winter storage and talk with several of the builders.

These visits confirmed my earlier research. Most of the custom lobster boats I examined were built by traditional boat builders in Maine with unique interiors finished at smaller custom shops. These smaller shops specialize in quality interior designs to fit the requirements of individual buyers.

I also learned more about skeg-built verses built-down lobster boat hull designs. The proponents of each style were certainly vocal about the benefits of their preferred design. Some buyers prefer the lighter skeg-built boats with their bolt-on keels and flat bottoms aft so they can run faster.

On the other hand, built-down, full-keel lobster boats run more efficiently at speeds in the mid-teens. They tend to be preferred by working fishermen and former cruising sailors switching to power. These owners prefer the sea-kindly motion, good balance and maneuverability provided by the built-down design.

My conversations with brokers and builders confirmed my earlier suspicions that it would save me a lot of time if I could locate an existing built-down boat for sale that met my interior design requirements.

At the end of the week I returned to Portland for my flight back to my home in New York.

4th Week of February

I dedicated the final week of February to finalizing the publication of Death Trap. A few proof copies had been printed in early February and distributed to selected friends, including Anne and Amanda. I had now incorporated most of their suggestions into the final book which would be published at the end of March.

#   #   #

Anne had been busy with her search and she called early Friday to report she had located several boats in Florida for me to consider. I returned to Fort Lauderdale on Saturday afternoon so we could spend the next week evaluating boats for sale in Fort Lauderdale, Miami and Palm Beach.

1st Week of March

Anne arranged for us to visit brokers in Fort Lauderdale on Sunday and Miami on Monday. On Tuesday we drove to Palm Beach and examined a Duffy 37 for sale, the same model as Anne's boat in Maine. I had been very impressed with the performance of Anne's boat the day she invited me to join her and the art students to view the schooner rendezvous in Maine.

This boat was several years newer than Anne's and it had a slightly different custom interior. Anne's experience with her boat certainly paid off and the broker quickly learned she was in charge of our evaluation.

At this stage I had rejected over a dozen boats posted for sale online. I had now looked at a dozen other boats in Maine and Florida but they all needed interior modifications. The interior design and arrangement of this boat was impressive.

The boat was designed for long-range cruising with extra refrigeration, an air conditioning & heating system, fully equipped galley, modern head with separate shower and extra storage in a stateroom with a queen bed. The main cabin had a custom desk with an Apple computer and entertainment system.

It was also equipped with satellite communications, a long-range WiFi and cell phone system and was already setup to add 5G cell phone capability. The boat's existing communications network provided everything I needed to work from the boat.

In addition, all the electronics and navigation systems were up-to-date, the main engine, generator and bow thruster all appeared to be in excellent condition. This was the best boat we had inspected to date.

On our drive back to Fort Lauderdale I told Anne I planned to make an offer to buy the boat. I was encouraged by Ken's support of my decision when we discussed my plan over drinks before dinner that evening.

Anne and I made another trip to Palm Beach the next day to examine the boat more closely before I made my offer to purchase.

Ken had arranged to have a broker help me negotiate a final price and by Friday we had finalized the contract, put my deposit in escrow and arranged for a sea trial the following week.

Ken also arranged for an experienced marine surveyor to do an independent evaluation of the boat's condition and a mechanic to evaluate the engine and generator. All this would occur when the current owner would take us out for the sea trial; a brief voyage in the open ocean to test all the boat's operating systems.

I was excited about the pending purchase and pleased Anne and I had been in agreement each step of the process. It was obvious we worked well together as I reflected on the week during my flight back to New York.

9

2nd Week of March

In mid-February, Brian McCoy, senior auditor at a bank in Palm Beach called me. He said the bank's board was requesting a cybersecurity briefing and a contact at the FBI suggested he call me. I told him it sounded interesting, and we scheduled my presentation for the bank's next board meeting scheduled on Tuesday morning the second week of March. This timing had made it possible for me to arrange the sea trial and survey the day after their board meeting.

My flight arrived in Palm Beach on Monday evening and I stayed overnight at a hotel near the bank in downtown West Palm Beach. I had never spent any time in West Palm and was impressed by my walk along the waterfront area and with the number of restaurants and shops along Clematis Street.

Tuesday morning I had a brief meeting with Darcy Levin, the bank's President, and Brian in her office before our meeting in the boardroom. The background information I obtained indicated Levin was about fifty and had been President for about five years. She worked for a large regional bank prior to being recruited by the bank's board to her current position.

The bank's dress code was less formal and I was overdressed in my suit and tie. Brian, a little shorter and heavier than me, was wearing a yellow long sleeve shirt with the bank's logo and khaki trousers.

Levin was about five and a half feet tall with short brunette hair. I would guess she was about average weight and looked more professional than Brian in her cream-colored pantsuit with a fitted jacket.

I enjoyed my discussion of cybersecurity risks with the board members and management team of this community bank. I was impressed with their personal knowledge and questions about the various risks related to unauthorized access into the bank's financial systems. About half my briefing discussed cybersecurity risks for various bank customers such as hotels, hospitals, schools, retail stores and personal devices. Cybersecurity is a critical function for all banks and difficult to manage at a small bank with limited resources.

Following the board meeting Levin asked me to join her in her office.

"Steve, we use first names at the bank and I would prefer you call me Darcy. I have another assignment for you if you are interested. It appears one of our bank's customers is involved in a global cryptocurrency fraud and I would like your opinion."

We arranged for me to return to the bank in two weeks. Based on my follow-up discussion with Darcy it appeared I could offer some helpful insights for bank management.

#   #   #

Anne picked me up at the bank's offices Tuesday evening and we returned to Fort Lauderdale to have dinner with the Stewarts. Our conversations that evening were all focused on the upcoming sea trial.

Anne drove me back to Palm Beach the next morning for the sea trial. We met my broker, the boat's owner, the boat owner's broker, the marine surveyor and the engine mechanic at Palm Harbor Marina. Following examination of the boat's systems at the dock, we all departed the Palm Beach inlet for an offshore test run to evaluate each system while underway.

It had become breezy and the ocean was becoming choppy, so the sea trial also provided a good test of the boat's handling characteristics in various sea conditions. Everything during the sea trial worked as expected and the verbal reports from the marine surveyor and mechanic were positive. Their official reports would be sent to me early Friday.

We arranged for the closing to take place Friday afternoon and for me to take delivery of my new boat that weekend at the Palm Harbor Marina in Palm Beach. Ken's broker made certain we covered every contingency and his guidance made my purchase a smooth transaction.

I wasn't prepared to answer when the seller's broker asked me what boat name they should put on the purchase and registration documents. After a short pause I said; "Paradox, let's name my new boat Paradox."

Paradox at Palm Harbor Marina

Few of my former banking colleagues knew about my interest in boating and I suspected they would all think I am experiencing a mid-life crisis.

On Saturday morning Anne and I took the train up to Palm Beach to meet my broker and take delivery of Paradox. I was excited as we walked down the dock and I spotted Paradox sitting snuggly in her slip.

The seller had removed all personal gear, and the boat was delivered in pristine condition. We had a busy weekend getting basic supplies aboard such as bedding, food, drinks, paper products and a few items from a marine store to prepare for our voyage back to Fort Lauderdale.

10

3rd Week of March

The Palm Beach Boat Show takes place at the Palm Harbor Marina the final week of March. As a result, we needed to move Paradox to Fort Lauderdale so the marina could accommodate yachts arriving for the upcoming show.

Fortunately, the ocean was calm late Monday morning for my first offshore voyage in Paradox. Anne and I departed the Palm Beach inlet and she helped me navigate the forty mile offshore voyage down the coast to Fort Lauderdale.

We entered Fort Lauderdale's Port Everglades inlet and navigated a short distance up the Intracoastal Waterway to a dock at the Bahia Mar Marina arriving about four hours after our departure from Palm Beach.

Bahia Mar is a resort complex on the Intracoastal Waterway across from Fort Lauderdale beach. The complex has restaurants, pools, shops - everything to keep a tourist entertained. It's also walking distance from a wide variety of restaurants.

I stayed aboard Paradox both day and night during the week to learn how the multitude of systems worked. A cruising boat like Paradox is its own self-contained entity with systems to provide all the comforts of home.

Anne arrived early each morning to start our daily navigation and operating lessons. Paradox had a GPS navigation system with a large screen for viewing navigation charts, radar, depth sounder and an autopilot. By the end of the week I felt comfortable operating my new powerboat alone - Anne was a competent instructor.

I prepared most of my meals onboard and Anne joined me several evenings for dinners. Her visits gave us an opportunity to talk.

"Anne, thanks for your help with Paradox. The interior arrangement is more comfortable than I expected and the technology provides more work and entertainment choices than I had imagined."

"The only significant change I've made is replacing the computer and installing software for a virtual private network and a sophisticated anti-virus program for work. It's clear I can both live and work from Paradox for extended periods of time."

My New Office on Paradox

4th Week of March

Monday morning I took the new high-speed train between Fort Lauderdale and Palm Beach for my meetings with Darcy and Brian.

One of the bank's customers was connected to a fraudulent international cryptocurrency operation. I worked with Brian and the bank's audit team on Monday and Tuesday to document the relationship for federal authorities.

Tuesday night I boarded a flight from Palm Beach to Kansas City to do a risk management briefing for another bank board. I hadn't initially appreciated how presentations at bank conferences established my reputation as a risk expert.

Wednesday night I took a flight to New York. I planned to spend the final days of March working on the initial marketing for Death Trap. My editor had sufficient connections and experience to arrange some press coverage and a few small book signings at independent bookstores over the weekend in New York.

1st Week of April

Tuesday morning I packed a new soft sided duffel for my return flight to Fort Lauderdale. I didn't have many appropriate clothes for the boat in New York and had started purchasing what I needed in Florida. My goal was to have everything needed on the boat so I could avoid packing and unpacking every trip between New York and Paradox.

On Wednesday Anne and I took Paradox offshore for the twenty nautical mile voyage to the Port of Miami for an overnight visit to Dinner Key Marina. We returned to Fort Lauderdale the next day as our objective was another training cruise not a vacation day in Miami.

I had now logged over two hundred miles of offshore cruising in Paradox and felt confident enough to plan a longer voyage to The Bahamas. Anne had chartered boats in The Bahamas on several occasions and we were both envious of Ken's vivid descriptions of cruising the turquoise waters of the Exuma Cays.

The weather forecast for the next week indicated light winds from the Southeast, ideal for crossing the Gulf Stream, the ocean current that runs between the coast of Florida and The Bahamas. We had no excuse not to go.

The Stewart's description of the Exuma Cays had wetted our appetite to cruise this hundred-mile long archipelago of 365 small cays and Islands located southeast of Nassau. We discussed our thoughts with Ken and Frances and they helped make arrangements for us to stay at Highbourne Cay, their favorite marina in the Exumas.

We spent the weekend provisioning for several weeks on Paradox as there are few places to buy fresh food and other supplies in the small, remote Out Islands of The Bahamas. It was essential we had all the supplies we would need on the boat when we started on our voyage.

11

2nd Week of April

We left Fort Lauderdale Monday morning, navigated fifty miles across the deep blue waters of the Gulf Stream and cleared Bahamian customs at Cat Cay. We had a Bahamian cracked conch dinner with island rum drinks that first night on the porch of a quaint restaurant overlooking the docks of this private island.

The next day we traveled eighty miles across the shallow Great Bahama Bank to Chub Cay. The banks are vast areas of shallow ocean water and it was unnerving for me to see sand and seaweed just a few feet below the keel of Paradox. The turquoise water over the shallow banks was as clear as the Stewart's swimming pool.

Chub Cay, a traditional sport fishing destination, is now a high-end resort with floating docks, private cottages and a large clubhouse with a swimming pool that overlooks a soft sand beach. We enjoyed the pool, had tropical rum drinks at the bar and I fixed a shrimp and pasta dinner for us on the boat.

We departed Chub Cay early Wednesday morning crossing the deep blue Tongue of the Ocean between Chub Cay and Nassau. We called Nassau Harbor Control late morning and received permission to navigate through busy Nassau Harbor passing several large hotels and massive cruise ships disembarking tourists at their docks.

As we departed Nassau Harbor, I was awestruck by the spectacular turquoise waters as we crossed the shallow Exuma Banks. We arrived at Highbourne Cay in late afternoon and entered their small well-protected marina that accommodates a couple of dozen yachts.

View from Highbourne Restaurant

Highbourne Cay is a very popular destination and reservations at this private island are essential. When we checked in at the small office it was clear

Ken's relationship made our visit possible.

Highbourne has four amazing white sand beaches around the cay and an excellent small restaurant with a view that overlooks the channel connecting deep Exuma Sound with the shallow Exuma Banks.

Each evening we strolled the docks with a glass of wine and visited with other folks visiting the marina on their boats. Everyone walking the docks was exceptionally relaxed and friendly. Our brief conversations were generally about the nice weather and wonderful facility. If names were shared, it was first name and boat name only.

After one friendly exchange I said; "That nice woman we just visited with looked really familiar."

Anne laughed and replied; "She should have - she just won an Oscar. She's apparently with friends on that large charter yacht at the dock."

Sharks at Highbourne

A favorite stop of ours was the fish cleaning station where we could admire a dozen sharks circling for scraps being tossed into the water. We were both relaxed and enjoyed sharing several romantic days together at Highbourne. I was determined to make this cay a return destination.

Highbourne Marina was completely booked for the weekend so early Saturday we ventured twenty-five miles south to the Exuma Land & Sea Park.

Exuma Park @ Paul Harding Photo

Exuma Park is known for its pristine beauty, dozens of undeveloped cays with outstanding anchorages and breathtaking marine environment. The Park is an official no fishing zone established seventy years ago to protect the marine environment. The Park's motto is "Take Only Photos - Leave Only Footprints".

We picked up a mooring at Warderick Wells, the undeveloped cay where the Park Ranger's Office is located. When visiting the small park office to pay for our mooring, we noticed Ken & Frances Stewart's names were on the plaque honoring major supporters of Exuma Park.

Paradox on Mooring at Exuma Park

We enjoyed a sunny weekend walking the trails, visiting secluded beaches and snorkeling colorful reefs to view the abundance of protected sea life. A weekend was insufficient time to truly appreciate the magical feeling of visiting this remote island. We were both entranced as we slowly ventured out the channel Monday morning.

Paradox: Voyage to The Bahamas

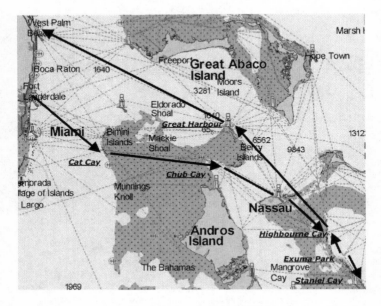

Navionics Screen Shot

12

3rd Week of April

Before leaving Florida, we arranged dockage at the Staniel Cay Yacht Club as our final destination in the Exuma Cays. The Club is near Thunderball Grotto and I wanted to visit the underwater cave where Keith Jones, the young banker from Maine, had died.

The Yacht Club is a small boutique resort with a few cottages, island 'honky tonk' bar and restaurant with docks for visiting yachts. It's a fun location and regular air service provided by a small island airline makes it easy for non-boaters, such as Keith Jones, to visit.

We arrived at the Yacht Club docks about mid-day Monday. That afternoon we rented a golf cart to explore the island's Bahamian community and the vacation houses built for visitors. We planned to eat dinner in Club's dining room our first night and joined the suntanned gathering at the busy bar prior to dinner being served.

I couldn't resist asking the bartender about the drowning tragedy. She was more than willing to share her opinion between stops to serve drinks to the growing crowd.

"Dumb, foolish, tourist! Nobody goes in Thunderball except at slack tide. Took the little boat that comes with the cottage over there late that night at the wrong time."

"Stupid to visit the cave at night. Damn lucky those kids found his body early the next morning. They said they were curious why one of our boats was tied to the mooring and sharks were circling the cave entrance. Damn lucky he wasn't shark bait."

"He was having a good time at our party earlier that night with the woman he was hanging out with. She was some classy gal - fancy dress and all - just disappeared - no idea who she was."

"Look for yourself - the pictures from our party are still up on the wall."

The time of death was news to me. The official report from the Bahamian authorities only stated that it was an accidental death by drowning in Thunderball Grotto.

Anne and I looked at one another, picked up our rum drinks and walked over to look at the pictures on the wall. I recognized the young banker from his obituary photo. Everyone was dressed island casual including the tall brunette next to the young banker. She looked like a fashion model on vacation - sexy tropical dress and beautiful. I used my cell phone to take a photo of one of the photos on the wall.

We also looked at old photos of Sean Connery and the movie cast for the James Bond movie Thunderball. This underwater cave was the location of several scenes and was renamed Thunderball in honor of the 1965 movie.

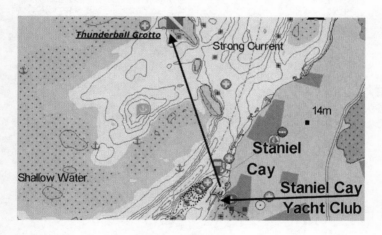

Yacht Club to Thunderball Grotto
Navionics Screen Shot

The underwater cave is less than a half-mile from the Yacht Club and I wanted to see the strong current described by the Cruising Guide. The next day, about two hours before low tide, we took my dinghy to circle the small cay where Thunderball Grotto is located to observe the strength of the outgoing tidal current.

Our Cruising Guide indicated Thunderball Grotto has two entrances and the direction the tidal current flows through the cave depends on the tide. There is a small mooring buoy used by small boats like my dinghy on the western side of the cay. Larger boats can anchor in the surrounding sandy seafloor.

Inside Thunderball Grotto

The Guide cautioned it's best to enter the cave at slack low tide with little current and the entrance is not below the surface of the water. Only strong swimmers are advised to enter Thunderball at slack high tide as they need to remain under water and swim below the ceiling of the cave entrance.

The tidal current was strong as we circled the small cay and, as we passed the mooring buoy, we could see the entrance was still below the surface of the water. It was foolish for Jones to enter the cave alone with an outgoing tide.

Anne and I returned two hours later and tied my dinghy to the buoy. We could easily enter and explore the cave for about thirty minutes at low tide. We were amazed at the marine life, colors of the surrounding rock formations and underwater coral. It's easy to see why Thunderball is a popular snorkeling destination for visiting boaters.

Our visit to Thunderball contributed to my curiosity about the young banker's death. Why would he visit the cave alone at night on an outgoing tide?

We spent the next day exploring the turquoise waters surrounding nearby cays in my dinghy. Many of these small cays with nice sandy beaches are undeveloped. A few cays had private homes surrounded by lovely vegetation and open decks overlooking sand beaches. We also passed a private island with a very large modern house that looked out of place in such a picturesque location.

Our visit by dinghy to Pig Beach on Big Major Cay revealed a unique tourist attraction. Several dozen boats, including four yachts much larger than the boat owned by the Stewarts, were anchored in a large protected cove off Pig Beach.

We were amused as tenders took guests from what we assumed were charter yachts to the beach to feed the pigs!

We suspected many of the visitors were city dwellers because the feeding technique we witnessed consisted of loud screams and running up and down the beach to avoid contact with a pig. Watching a pig swim by our dinghy was far better than joining the chaos on the beach.

Swimming Pig at Big Major Cay

\#   \#   \#

The weather along the coast of Florida was changing as the time approached for our return voyage. Any north wind across the Gulf Stream builds very rough wave conditions. I decided to play it safe and keep Paradox in The Bahamas.

I contacted Ken to ask if he could arrange for me to keep Paradox at Highbourne Cay for the next several weeks. Thankfully, he could make arrangements and we departed Staniel Cay on Thursday morning and headed north to Highbourne.

Returning to the more relaxed atmosphere at Highbourne was truly enjoyable. I could easily understand why Ken told us Highbourne is their favorite destination in The Bahamas. We observed a marvelous red sunset over the Exuma Banks as we savored our last conch salad dinner on the deck at the Highbourne restaurant.

Ken arranged for us to charter a small seaplane on Sunday morning for the short flight to Nassau and a commercial flight back to Fort Lauderdale.

Seaplane at Highbourne Cay

13

4th Week of April

Anne and I boarded our flight to Bangor on Tuesday morning and I rented a car to drive us to Stone Harbor so Anne could start getting her Inn ready for the summer tourist season. I offered to help, but when we arrived it was clear Anne had everything under control and my presence was mostly a distraction. As before, when Anne was working at her Inn our relationship was more businesslike than personal.

I decided it was best for me to return to my apartment in New York to work on my book promotion. I booked my flight out of Portland so I could check-in with James Parker at the bank on my return to New York. When I called to arrange a time to meet, he offered to take Amanda and me to dinner in appreciation for the help we had provided. James was accompanied by his wife and we enjoyed a delightful evening together at a first-class waterfront restaurant overlooking the harbor.

As we walked out of the restaurant after dinner, James stopped to talk to two couples at another table. He briefly introduced us to be polite and then we departed. As we waited for the valet to deliver our cars, I asked;

"James, did you say that man's name was Robert Alexander? Is that the attorney associated with the law firm that had the two accounts we questioned at the Rockland branch?"

He responded as the valet delivered his car; "Yes, that was Robert. He has a very successful law firm."

Amanda's car was next in line and we started back to my hotel. Amanda always arranged to drive so once again I had no idea where she lived.

On the way back to the hotel she said; "I didn't know you had an interest in Alexander's law firm."

"I was just curious why his firm had a couple of large accounts at the Rockland branch. I asked Tory to do some follow-up and she was told Alexander's son was a college classmate of Jones. Apparently, the accounts had been opened as a favor to help Jones win a new account contest and they were closed shortly after his death. I found it surprising the law firm didn't have a website."

Amanda volunteered; "Alexander's firm specializes

in personal injury cases. They used to have those obnoxious ads about winning money if you were hurt. Thankfully, Maine doesn't have those large billboards along the roads like most other states!"

She continued; "I would guess it was about ten years ago when Alexander won a big settlement in a medical malpractice lawsuit that got him a lot of publicity. That settlement made the firm famous, and they stopped the obnoxious advertising."

We arrived at my hotel and as Amanda departed, she said; "Good night Steve, as always, I enjoyed the evening with you."

14

1st Week of May

My flight from New York landed mid-day in Nassau where I was scheduled to meet an experienced crew member arranged by Ken Stewart. Ken's contacts were invaluable and a young man in his twenties was waiting for me in the airport lobby. We took a taxi around the airport to the private aircraft terminal and boarded the seaplane I chartered to fly us to Highbourne. My plan this trip was to take Paradox from Highbourne to the Palm Harbor Marina in Palm Beach.

I had received a call in mid-April from Darcy Levin, President of the bank in Palm Beach, asking for help concerning a possible fraud. As a result, I made a reservation to return to the marina for several weeks and planned to stay aboard Paradox while I worked on the bank's project.

Palm Harbor Marina is located along the West Palm Beach waterfront and is walking distance to both the bank's headquarters building and dozens of restaurants in the Clematis entertainment district. The marina has security gates, floating docks and a comfortable lounge with a well-equipped fitness center for my morning exercise. The lounge overlooks the yacht harbor and has a fully equipped business center. Restaurants and shopping are within walking distance to the marina so I made no plans to rent a car.

Palm Harbor Marina & West Palm Beach

We departed Highbourne on Paradox early Wednesday morning and navigated a longer more northerly route on the voyage back to Florida. The seas were smooth but our return voyage was not a leisurely pleasure cruise. We only made one overnight stop on Wednesday night at Great Harbour Marina in the Berry Islands.

We arrived in Palm Beach Thursday evening and my temporary crew member took the train back to Fort Lauderdale. I enjoyed the weekend being back on Paradox at Palm Harbor Marina and exploring the West Palm Beach waterfront.

2nd Week of May

On Monday morning I found myself back in a familiar conference room at the bank reviewing personal accounts for a woman named Pamala Jenkins. Brian McCoy did not provide any background as he wanted me to take a fresh look and draw my own conclusions. I didn't know why the accounts might be considered suspicious and, other than rather large monthly deposits, they just appeared to be personal accounts for the monthly expenses of a wealthy woman.

Darcy then arranged for the two of us to have a private lunch and, once seated, she asked;

"What do you think?"

I responded; "Everything looks fine. The woman's new account information indicates she has an inheritance held in trust by a Chicago bank and the bank sends her eighty thousand dollars each month by wire transfer. She appears to manage her money responsibly and provides generous support to local charity events. Why are you concerned?"

"Several weeks ago while having lunch at my golf club I overheard two men talking about their investment returns. One fellow was bragging that his money manager was producing consistent annual returns of twelve percent or more and he was receiving a check every month to supplement his retirement. His friend was obviously envious and asked if he could invest with the same manager."

"It was his answer that disturbed me. He said, 'My investment manager's technique is proprietary, and I am required to keep our arrangement confidential. I can't tell you more but I guess I could ask her if the manager would take another account'."

"His friend was persistent, and he finally said, 'Please don't tell anyone but Pamala Jenkins arranged for me to open my account with her investment manager'."

Darcy added; "I have lived in Florida long enough to smell a scam and 'too good to be true' is still a good indicator. As you know, the markets have been experiencing historic volatility and consistent returns of any kind are suspect. Their conversation reminded me of the Madoff Ponzi scheme uncovered a few years ago."

"I am socially acquainted with Pamala and she has several accounts with our bank. I want to make certain no one at the bank is doing anything wrong. I don't like what I overheard at the club. I want to know what the bank might need to do if this could be some kind of scam."

As we finished lunch I asked; "Do you know the name of the man at the club who has the account with Jenkins?"

"Yes, his name is Howard Adams III."

After lunch I returned to that familiar conference room to discuss Adams's account relationships with Brian.

The only account relationship we identified was a personal checking account apparently used by Adams and his wife for household expenses. Money for these household expenses was provided by occasional wire transfers from a personal account Adams had at a bank in New York.

I took a few minutes at the end of the day to tell Darcy I saw no evidence that her bank was associated with a fraud. However, I agreed the investment return Adams discussed with his friend was certainly suspicious. We agreed she would call me if anything new surfaced with the accounts related to Jenkins or Adams.

#   #   #

Tuesday afternoon Darcy called and asked me to meet her in her office. When I arrived she said; "You will not believe what happened this morning. Howard Adams requested a short-term loan to buy a yacht."

"He told me his primary banking relationship is with the bank in New York but, since we advertise boat loans, he thought he should talk to us first. He thought it might be easier to arrange a ninety-day loan for three million dollars until he could withdraw the funds from an investment account."

"We specialize in boat loans so I am interested in lending him the money. I told him we would be happy to consider the loan. I explained we normally take the boat as collateral, charge a fee to cover the yacht registration paperwork and require at least a five-year term to make the loan worthwhile for the bank."

"Howard responded he wasn't really interested in a long-term boat loan and had already deposited three million in the broker's escrow account for the purchase of the yacht. He explained he was requesting the short-term loan because his investment account requires a ninety-day notice for withdrawals and he suggested he offer his investment account as collateral. He told me he would bring a copy of his investment statement to my office tomorrow morning."

I asked; "Did Howard tell you the name of this investment account?"

Darcy replied; "No, he just said he would bring me his last statement tomorrow. I will let you know if it is the account related to Jenkins."

I also asked; "What do you know about Howard?"

I understand his wife inherited a family business several years ago they sold for a significant amount of money. I don't think he has any real business or investment experience. He and his wife moved to Palm Beach about five years ago. I only know him from the golf club and before yesterday I didn't even know they had a personal checking account at the bank.

#   #   #

Wednesday afternoon Darcy called again and asked me to come to her office. When I arrived she placed a single page investment statement on her desk in front of me.

After a quick review, I asked; "Are you going to lend him the money to buy a yacht based on this statement?"

"No, not with this account as collateral."

"So, what next?"

"His boat purchase is bankable on its own. He also brought in the paperwork for the purchase and he has already deposited three million dollars in the brokerage escrow account for a six million dollar yacht purchase."

I asked; "Isn't that a lot of money to put in a boat escrow? I only did a few thousand for my boat."

Darcy replied; "I told you I didn't think he had much business experience. I suspect he was trying to impress the broker. In any event, we can do a simple assignment of title for the yacht and convert it to a more traditional loan if he doesn't withdraw the funds from this investment account."

I asked; "What about this investment account?"

Darcy responded with a question; "What do you think?"

I was perplexed; "I am not sure what to say - I have never seen such a limited statement - it provides no meaningful information."

"The only information printed on this statement is Trust Account - Howard Adams, Proprietary Investment Fund with an account number. This statement provides no investment manager name or contact information. No detailed investment or securities information is listed for the twenty-five million dollar account balance. I have no idea who manages his money or what securities, if any, might be in his account."

"How did Howard explain this?"

Darcy responded; "That's why I called you."

"Howard said Pamala has her money invested in the same proprietary investment program and she explained the investment manager requires his investment technique remain confidential. As a result, the manager doesn't disclose the actual transactions, just the results. The objective of the investment technique is to maintain a fairly steady account balance that produces a steady return of twelve percent or more annually with a custom mix of dividends, interest and capital gains."

Darcy added; "I was disturbed by his answer when I asked if he had any more detail about the account. He said; 'I thought you would understand - my monthly checks come from your bank'."

15

Thursday morning Brian and I returned to the conference room and discussed how we should proceed. Brian told me he had checked again, and the bank had no other personal account relationships and no trust account for Howard Adams or his wife.

We still had the copy of Adams's investment account which indicated he was earning about a twelve percent return and receiving around three million dollars in cash distributions each year. I estimated that was about double the cash flow that would be expected in a more traditional account. An extra million dollars or more a year would be a good reason for Adams to respect the investment manager's requirement to keep the account relationship confidential.

His investment statement indicated the monthly check from his trust account was dated the fifth of each month and his last check was for $250,000. However, no deposit for that amount appeared on the last several statements for his personal account at the bank. All the deposits for the past several months to his personal account had been wire transfers from his personal account at the bank in New York.

Brian asked; "What next? Do we ask him for a copy of one of the trust account checks he indicated had been sent to him by the bank?"

I responded; "No, I learned long ago we do not want to prematurely expose our interest in a possible fraud - it only gives the perpetrators an opportunity to cover their tracks and potentially disappear. I suggested we work backwards and check his deposits for the prior year."

We located a check in the amount of $250,000 deposited to his personal account in November. The image of the deposit showed it was from an account at the bank in Palm Beach named 'Proprietary Investment Account' and it was signed by a Sally McDonald. Now that we knew the name of the account at the bank we could review the statements and identify all the checks issued to Adams.

A short while later, Brian reported; "Monthly checks are issued to Adams and six other individuals from the same Proprietary Investment Account. The account only has a small balance after all the checks are cashed. New funds arrived monthly by wire transfer from a bank in Chicago a few days before the checks were issued."

I noted the information on the wire transfer indicated the funds came from the same account that wired the monthly deposits to Pamala Jenkins.

"Brian, these transactions are certainly suspicious but they could be legitimate transfers from individual investment accounts managed by the same investment manager. We are at a dead-end without information on the original source of funds from the bank in Chicago."

Expanding our inquiry raised numerous legal and privacy issues and we did not want to do anything that would alert Jenkins. I walked back to my boat that night with lots of questions and no answers. The next morning I called Mark to ask for advice.

Mark listened to my briefing without asking questions. He then summarized;

"These transactions certainly sound suspicious given the investment returns being reported."

"You used the wire transfer information to identify the bank in Chicago sending the funds to Palm Beach. We both know the senior auditor at that bank - why not call her? Tell her you want to discuss a possible fraud and ask to meet?"

"Steve, your client's customer, has requested a

bank loan based on monthly payments coming from an account at her bank in Chicago. You can ask her to confirm that Adams has a trust account at the bank or confirm those funds are coming from a legitimate investment account."

I planned to return home to New York on Friday and arranged for a stopover in Chicago. Due to my suspicions, I wanted to have this conversation face-to-face and arranged to have lunch with the senior auditor at the bank in Chicago.

16

3rd Week of May

Monday afternoon the following week I got a call from the auditor in Chicago; "Steve, our bank does not have a trust account or, for that matter, any accounts with Howard Adams. The account you asked about was opened by a Sally McDonald. The money for that account arrives by wire transfer from some type of investment firm with an account at a bank in Charlotte."

I called Mark and reported the results of my inquiry. We both agreed the transactions were very suspicious as funds from legitimate trust accounts would not be commingled.

Mark concluded; "Steve, my team in Florida is already understaffed and is currently investigating a large drug related money laundering operation based in Miami. As a result, I need to assign other agents to new cases. It will help if you would return to Palm Beach and help us with this case."

I returned to Paradox in Palm Beach Tuesday afternoon. Mark's suggestion presented a unique situation for me. My bank client appeared to be a conduit for an investment fraud. At the same time, Mark was now asking me to establish an official consulting relationship with the FBI so I could assist with the investigation. I discussed this possible conflict of interest with Darcy, the bank's attorneys and an attorney at the FBI. Thankfully, we reached an agreement that respected the interests of both the bank and the FBI.

This arrangement placed me in a rather awkward position. As a consultant to the bank I was able to examine certain customer information subject to their confidentiality requirements that I could not disclose to the FBI without a court order. On the other hand, I could examine other information gathered by the FBI that was not available to the bank. This arrangement placed me in a unique position to more quickly unravel the transactions that we suspected of being related to an investment fraud.

I wasn't really surprised when Amanda called me Wednesday; "Steve, Mark asked me to review this possible case. You didn't learn much of value from the Chicago bank. The account that was used to transfer money to Palm Beach was also just a clearing account. What do you think?"

I responded: "Pamala Jenkins doesn't say she is an investment manager and the accounts indicate no relationship between Jenkins, the bank in Chicago or the investment firm in Charlotte. The accounts in Palm Beach and Chicago were both opened by a Sally McDonald. Furthermore, I checked with the Securities & Exchange Commission and they have no record of a registered investment firm by that name."

"The account in Palm Beach was opened about four years ago by a Sally McDonald with a five thousand dollar wire transfer from the account at the bank in Chicago. The next deposit was a couple of weeks later for five million dollars from Howard Adams. His deposit was transferred to the account at the bank in Chicago the next day."

"The first checks from the Palm Beach account were issued to Adams a month later. We have also discovered four more deposits from Adams for five million dollars each so his total investment in his so-called trust account is now twenty-five million dollars. I guess his wife sold that family business for a tidy sum."

"Amanda, over the past three years about six million dollars has been sent from that account in Chicago back to the Proprietary Investment Account in Palm Beach for payments to Adams."

"We have also identified deposits from six more

individuals and they are also receiving monthly checks from this same Proprietary Investment Account. A total of ninety-five million dollars has now been deposited into this Palm Beach account and subsequently transferred to the bank in Chicago."

"All the deposits were made to the Proprietary Investment Account with a notation on each deposit that the funds were to be further invested in that client's individual trust account. However, no such trust accounts were established at either the bank in Palm Beach or Chicago."

"What is missing in my analysis is any indication that any of the ninety-five million dollars has been placed in any type of investment or trust account. I am only looking at numerous wire transfers between the two banks and none of the accounts have any significant balances."

The missing link between the accounts was the transfers to the mysterious investment firm in Charlotte. However, Amanda and I could locate no website or regulatory information for a firm of that name. To my surprise, my online search of a Charlotte Business Directory did list a firm by that name at an office building in suburban Charlotte.

"Amanda, I suggest we meet in Charlotte Friday morning to visit this office building. We can just walk in and I will say I am interested in opening an account. I will use my identification and introduce you as my assistant so you don't have to provide identification and we can avoid disclosing you are an agent. We need some first-hand knowledge to learn more about this mysterious investment firm. Let's plan to meet in Charlotte Friday morning and see what happens."

# # #

When we arrived at the Charlotte airport I was wearing a traditional blue sport coat, khaki slacks and a blue dress shirt without a tie. Amanda arrived with her blonde hair up, wearing a conservative pale blue pantsuit I had never seen. She certainly changed her college student appearance for our trip to Charlotte. We arrived in time for a quick lunch at the airport and then took a short taxi ride to the suburban office building.

The directory in the lobby indicated the investment firm's office was located on the fifth floor. When we exited the elevator, we entered a common reception area for multiple business organizations with security doors protecting the entrance to each hallway leading to individual offices. I approached the receptionist and introduced myself:

"Good morning, my name is Steve Wilson."

She was very official and replied; "May I see some identification please?"

I provided a copy of my driver's license and she made a note of my name and confirmed the name of the firm I had asked to visit.

"The office is just down that hall on your left but no one is there today. In fact, I haven't seen anybody for a couple of weeks."

I improvised; "Gee, that's a surprise! I thought we were scheduled to come in today to review our account. When does he come to the office?"

The receptionist suspiciously replied; "Him? Don't you mean her? She's the only one I see when she visits the office about once a month to pick up mail."

I responded; "I thought Ralph also worked out of this office."

"Never heard of him. Ms. Jenkins is the only person I know."

"OK, thanks, guess I was confused."

As Amanda and I walked back toward the elevator, she stopped and said; "Wait here."

Amanda returned to the receptionist's desk and whispered something to the receptionist. Amanda looked my direction and said; "Be right back."

The receptionist then clicked open the lock on one of the security doors and Amanda walked into the hallway leading to the interior offices.

A short while later Amanda walked back out, said "Thank You" to the receptionist and joined me for the elevator ride down.

"Amanda, what was that about?"

"I thought it was worth a chance to look at the office. I simply smiled and asked the receptionist if I could use the ladies' room. Told her I hate to stop at a gas station. She said she understood and directed me through the door and down the hallway."

"I located the firm's office and looked through a glass panel next to the locked door. There is a desk and chair just like in a couple of empty offices I passed - that is all. That office is empty except for a little mail sitting on top of the desk."

"The office next door is occupied by an insurance salesman. Pushy guy came out to flirt with me."

He said; "Can I help you? She never shows up at her office and when she does, she isn't very friendly."

Amanda added; "We can skip the rest of his comments."

"Steve, it was certainly worthwhile to visit Charlotte - this is definitely not a legitimate investment firm."

I was impressed; "Amanda, that was good thinking on your part; I was on my way out of the building."

"Thanks, now let's tell the driver to drop us off at a Starbucks. I would like a cappuccino and I was too busy to use the bathroom."

The weather was pleasant, so we sat outside at a table to drink our coffee before returning to the airport to return to Palm Beach and Portland.

Amanda gave me a serious look on our taxi ride to the airport and said; "Your comment to the receptionist was interesting."

"Which comment?"

"I was caught off-guard when you referred to us as a couple. I thought I was your assistant."

"Just seemed like the thing to do at the time."

17

4th Week of May - Memorial Day

Amanda arrived in Palm Beach Tuesday morning to manage the investigation and we discussed steps to close the circle around Pamala Jenkins. However, the inquiries at both banks confirmed all the wire transfers for each of the accounts we had identified were authorized by a person named Sally McDonald.

It appeared all the accounts had been established by and were controlled by this Sally McDonald. The only connection to Jenkins was the comment from the receptionist in Charlotte. It was time to learn about the relationship between Jenkins and McDonald.

Amanda started compiling background reports from public records on Jenkins and women named Sally McDonald in Palm Beach. Jenkins was in her mid-40s and appeared to be single. She lived across the bridge in an exclusive apartment building in Palm Beach.

Jenkins appeared in numerous photos of charitable events where we suspected she networked with potential clients. She had a degree in finance from a prominent university in New England and had worked as a broker with several registered investment firms in both New York and Charlotte. It appeared she had moved to Palm Beach about four years ago. There was nothing in her background to indicate how she accumulated her apparent wealth. A Palm Beach Social Directory listed an office and phone number for Jenkins at an address near Worth Avenue.

Sally McDonald was more difficult to identify. Amanda located several dozen women with variations of the name who lived in the area. I took a shortcut and checked the bank records and located a copy of the driver's license that had been used to open the Proprietary Investment Account. The photo was not Jenkins but the address on the driver's license was the same as the address for Jenkins's office across the bridge in Palm Beach.

This information did not help us identify McDonald. The Florida driver's license information had a photo but we had no home address or other information for Sally McDonald.

It was time to learn more. I made an appointment to meet Jenkins at her office Wednesday afternoon.

#   #   #

Jenkins's office was located in a small but very tasteful building in the Mizner architectural style. Her office was a short walk from Worth Avenue on the Palm Beach side of the Intracoastal Waterway.

When I set up my appointment, I had only told her secretary I wanted to visit about an upcoming charitable event.

This was partially true. As a cover, Darcy had volunteered me to help with a charitable dinner being arranged at the Breakers, a historic hotel that hosted many of the high-end charitable events in Palm Beach.

When I arrived at her office, the sign on the door just said 'Pamala Jenkins' and when I entered her small reception area I was greeted by;

"Good afternoon, I am Sally McDonald, Pamala's assistant. Please have a seat, she is on the phone. Can I offer you a cup of coffee or something else to drink?"

I replied; "Thank you, no."

My first impression was this could have been the office of an attorney as no investment material or equipment was visible. McDonald had a small laptop on her desk but it was otherwise clear of any papers. The only magazines on the small side table were glossy social publications for Palm

Beach and the pictures on the walls were all tropical scenes.

A minute later, a rather tall, very stylish brunette dressed in a fitted black woman's business suit entered the room. "Hi, please call me Pamala. Come in."

Pamala's office resembled the outer office with similar artwork on the walls and a smaller desk that looked as if it could be an antique. She had a small laptop and a closed leather folder on her desk. She invited me to sit in a comfortable chair next to a small coffee table graced with a Robb Report.

Jenkins sat in a matching chair and opened the conversation.

"I understand from my assistant you work with Darcy over at the bank. Is it OK if I call you Steve?"

Jenkins had a friendly smile and a very charming personality. I could easily see how she could persuade someone she was doing them a favor if her investment manager accepted them as a new client. After some small talk about the nice weather, I asked for her support for the charitable dinner. Without hesitation she offered to buy a table and promised to invite people that had the financial capacity to support the event.

I then changed the subject and tried to look confused; "Your office is not what I expected, I thought you were doing something with investments."

Without hesitation she replied; "Oh no, I do a little on my own but I have most of my money invested with a very successful money manager. He makes it possible for me to live comfortably on my inheritance."

I replied; "Gee, I wish I had a money manager like that! Does he take new accounts?"

She chuckled; "No, I believe his fund is closed to new investments and anyway I understand the minimum account is now five million dollars."

"Ouch, that's a bit rich for me. Thanks for your time and the donation. It's greatly appreciated."

#   #   #

Amanda was also working on other cases while she was assigned to the FBI office in Palm Beach to manage the Jenkins investigation. We met later that afternoon at her temporary office and I briefed her on my meeting with Jenkins.

I concluded by saying; "It appears the entire scheme is managed by Jenkins. I see no sign of any investment manager or actual investment accounts for any of these clients. She has her assistant, Sally McDonald, set up the accounts and authorize the transactions. It appears Jenkins is very careful to keep her name out of the loop."

Amanda observed; "Very clever - she doesn't tell people she manages the money so they don't push her for any details. She creates confidence by saying she has also invested her money with this fictitious investment manager. We know the clients' checks are written to the Proprietary Investment Account, so it doesn't appear to the investors that any of the money is going to Jenkins."

Amanda asked my opinion of McDonald and I replied;

"I really have no opinion - we just met in passing. I can't even describe her as anything but average - she just wasn't memorable."

Amanda asked; "What next?"

I replied; "How about dinner? Let's talk about this tomorrow."

Like many business folks working away from home we found dinner to be a convenient way to relax at the end of a busy day. That night we walked to a casual hamburger joint on Clematis Avenue. After dinner I again walked back to my boat at the marina and Amanda returned to her hotel.

#   #   #

Thursday morning we called Mark to bring him up-to-date. We reviewed the diagram of accounts and transactions we had prepared that illustrated the flow of funds between the various accounts. We had identified ninety-five million dollars of deposits into the Proprietary Investment Account at the bank in Palm Beach and about fifteen million dollars of payments to seven clients from that same account. The monthly payments wired to Jenkins from the bank in Chicago totaled five million dollars.

However, we were at a dead-end in Charlotte and had identified no accounts with a significant amount of money. We had hoped to locate the missing seventy-five million dollars and take steps to freeze all the accounts at the same time we initiated legal action.

I suggested I meet with the senior audit executive at the Charlotte bank. My contact at the Chicago bank had given us the information required to diagram the flow of funds between the two banks and the so-called clients. An additional conversation with the bank in Charlotte might provide the information we needed to track the remaining seventy-five million dollars and confirm our suspicions.

I was acquainted with the bank's senior auditor

and arranged a flight to Charlotte to meet him on Friday to explain our suspicions. I suggested he conduct an internal review of the investment firm and its accounts and, if the transactions looked suspicious, contact Amanda at the FBI.

18

1st Week of June

Amanda had returned to Maine over the weekend and she planned to work for a few days in Portland. The weather was hot but clear in Florida and I spent the weekend practicing my docking skills.

I wanted to tune up my boating skills as Anne had invited me to return to Stone Harbor so we could spend a week cruising in her boat along the coast of Maine. I hoped Anne would be relaxed on the boat and our time together would be enjoyable away from her duties at the Inn.

Amanda called Tuesday morning with bad news.

"Steve, the auditor from Charlotte called me about an hour ago. The investment firm's account is located in the bank's branch office we noticed in the office building when we visited. However, like the other accounts all but a few thousand dollars has been transferred out of that account and this won't be so easy to track - seventy million dollars has been systematically wired to a numbered account in Switzerland. Over the past four years McDonald has wired a total of five million dollars to her account at a bank in Miami."

I asked; "What's next?"

"I called Mark, and we have decided it's time to act. We had hoped to locate most of the money and freeze the accounts before acting so we could recover the maximum amount of money for the investors. That's just not possible on a timely basis if the money is in Switzerland."

"I plan to return to Palm Beach to help our attorneys finalize the evidence we have accumulated and let them decide the next steps. I obviously want your help."

Amanda arrived late Wednesday and the balance of the week, including most of the weekend, was spent working together in a conference room at the FBI office documenting the evidence for the attorneys to present to a judge on Monday.

2nd Week of June

I completed my analysis over the weekend and prepared a summary for the attorneys to present to the judge. My summary illustrated how the ninety-five million dollars invested by the clients had been systematically wired by McDonald to the account in Chicago and then to the account in Charlotte. None of the funds were invested for the benefit of clients. Fifteen million dollars of the clients own money was returned as 'investment income' to create the appearance of a successful investment program that would, in turn, lure more people to invest more money in their scam.

Jenkins Case: Wire Transfer Summary ($000)		
7 'Clients': Hypothetical Investment Accounts	$95,000	$15,000
	V	∧
Proprietary Account: Bank in Palm Beach	$95,000	$15,000
	V	∧
Wire Transfers: Palm Beach to Chicago	$95,000	∧
Wire Transfers: Chicago to Palm Beach	V	$15,000
	V	∧
Proprietary Account: Bank in Chicago	$95,000	$15,000
	V	∧
Wire Transfers: Chicago to Charlotte	$95,000	∧
Wire Transfers: Charlotte to Chicago	V	$15,000
	V	∧
Fictitious Investment Firm: Charlotte	$95,000 >	$15,000
	V	
Wired to Bank in Switzerland	($70,000)	
Wired to Chicago/Palm Beach: Jenkins	($5,000)	
Wired to Miami: McDonald Account	($5,000)	
Remaining Funds	$0	

The Palm Beach bank's records indicated that the checks from the Proprietary Investment Account written to the Palm Beach investors had always been dated the 5th of the month and cleared within a few days. I planned to include last week's payments as part of our evidence for the court.

However, I discovered no money had been transferred into the account the prior week. To my alarm Darcy called me a few minutes later.

"Steve, Howard Adams called me asking why his check had been delayed by the bank. He said he had just talked to Jenkins on the phone and she told him she had not yet received her check. She assumed the bank's delay had something to do with the timing of the weekend. I am concerned that Jenkins is blaming our bank for the delay in issuing the checks. Our bank has nothing to do with these payments."

This change in pattern alarmed me and I immediately called Amanda at the FBI office.

"Amanda, something is wrong. No money was transferred last week for the monthly payments to Adams or the other clients. I think you need to tell your legal team to move quickly."

"I'm taking a taxi over to Jenkins's office to see if she and McDonald are still there. I can always pretend I want to thank Jenkins for her charitable donation."

I arrived at her office shortly before noon and was relieved to see the entrance door was unlocked. I casually walked in and said; "Hello".

McDonald was not at her desk but I could hear

movement behind the door into the private office.

So I knocked and said; "Ms. Jenkins?"

A voice responded; "Yes?"

"It's Steve Wilson, I stopped by to thank you for your contribution to the event."

It was silent for a moment, then the door opened and I was facing a furious Jenkins. She looked around to make certain I was alone and produced a small revolver she was holding behind her back. She motioned me into her office; "Come in and sit down!"

"I should have suspected trouble when they said a Steve Wilson stopped by the office in Charlotte. Now with no warning that bitch has deserted me and you walk in my office! I need a little time so give me your cell phone."

"Now, get up and step in that closet. Keep your mouth shut."

The closet was tight and I could barely move. It was pitch black when she pushed the door closed and I heard a key turn the lock. I could hear activity a few more minutes and then the office was quiet. I was increasingly claustrophobic but waited until I was certain Jenkins was gone before I started shouting - to no avail.

I was locked in the tiny closet for what seemed like an eternity when I heard the distinctive ring of my cell phone out in the office. I was relieved to hear my ring and hoped it was Amanda checking on me and not a robocall offering me a free weekend at a theme park.

It seemed another eternity passed as I anxiously awaited any sound in the office. It was a relief to hear a familiar voice calling; "Ms. Jenkins?"

I had almost lost my voice from my earlier shouting but managed; "Amanda, I'm locked in the closet!"

Amanda replied; "Steve? How the hell did you get in there? Damn, the closet door is locked with a key. Let me look for the keys and I will also call our team for a locksmith."

Fortunately, a few minutes later I heard her say; "I found a set of keys in the wastebasket. Give me a minute."

Amanda tried several keys and then the door opened. The sudden light made me dizzy, and I stumbled out. Amanda gave me a big hug;

"I got worried when you didn't call after being gone over two hours. It was time to check on you when you didn't answer your phone or return my call. What the hell happened?"

# # #

Once I regained my composure, we returned to Amanda's office and the prosecutors debriefed me.

"Somehow Jenkins was tipped off, and she is armed and on the run. I don't know if she's dangerous but an angry woman with a gun scares the hell out of me."

# # #

At the end of my debriefing Amanda turned;

"Steve, you need a drink. It's my turn to take you to dinner - tonight is not 'Dutch'. I will meet you at Pistache at 7:30."

This was my first time to have dinner at Pistache, an upscale French Bistro in the Clematis area of West Palm. I had walked by the restaurant numerous times as it's just a short walk from the marina. I arrived early to wait for Amanda. She had made a reservation, and I was quickly seated at our table.

I almost didn't recognize Amanda when she walked in the restaurant. The way a woman styles her hair and the outfit she wears can make a dramatic difference in appearance. Amanda almost always had her hair in a ponytail and this was the first time I had seen her with her long blonde hair down over her shoulders. She had also traded her signature jeans for a very stylish long blue dress that certainly accented her figure. I wasn't the only person who noticed her entrance.

As she approached our table, I stood and smiled; "You look amazing!"

Amanda blushed a little and offered a very gracious; "Thank you."

The menu at Pistache offered a wide variety of choices and we selected calamari for an appetizer and the lobster special for our dinners. We ordered a bottle of Pinot Grigio and avoided conversation about the pending case. Our dinner selection prompted Amanda to ask detailed questions about my selection of a lobster boat.

Her questions prompted me to ask; "Amanda, you ask really insightful questions. How do you know so much about lobster boats?"

She replied; "Steve, you are great when asking questions about a case but you seem very respectful of my privacy. I don't mind sharing personal information with you. Thanks for asking."

"Several of my relatives own and work lobster boats. I worked as crew for several summers during college for my uncle and we hauled traps in all kinds of weather."

Amanda gave me a look while we were sipping our cappuccinos after dinner and said; "Steve, you are staring and it's not at me. What's up?"

"Sorry, a woman that just departed looked familiar. I thought she might be the woman in the photo with Keith Jones, the banker from Maine."

"What are you talking about? What photo?"

"Never mind. I saw a photo of Keith with a woman at Staniel Cay in The Bahamas when I visited on my boat in April. I'm not at all certain that was her. Let's not spoil a nice evening with shop talk."

After dinner I waited outside with Amanda until the valet brought her rental car around to her. I was delighted she gave me a big smile and affectionate hug before she drove away. I walked slowly back to the marina and Paradox, very happy to be freed from a claustrophobic closet by a clever woman.

19

I packed my travel bag and departed for my flight to Bangor and Stone Harbor on Thursday morning.

Anne was busy at the Inn getting prepared for the arrival of tourists in early July when I arrived. I enjoyed two days walking around town and visiting with local folks I had met the prior year.

3rd Week of June

June is not the best cruising time in Maine since it's still cool with frequent fog and rain. However, Anne needed to go on our cruise before the Inn got busy in July.

On Sunday morning, Anne and I started our planned voyage along the coast. We only had light morning fog and picked up a mooring at Center Harbor, home of the Brooklin Boat Yard, where Anne stores her boat for the winter. The first night we walked up to the Brooklin Inn for drinks at their Pub and dinner in the restaurant. It was a very nice evening but Anne was preoccupied evaluating how another Inn was organized and managed. We were both tired and sleep came easily as the boat rocked gently on her mooring.

Center Harbor at Brooklin Boat Yard

The next morning we enjoyed eggs, bacon and coffee onboard as we waited for the morning fog to lift. We then headed to the Front Street Shipyard to spend the next two days exploring Belfast. The opening of this facility a few years ago has had a dramatic and positive impact on the Belfast waterfront. The light rain and fog in the mornings had no impact on our afternoon walks and evening dinners along the waterfront. As we both began to relax our time together became more enjoyable.

Thursday morning was bright and clear and we took advantage of calm seas to cruise down the coast to the Boothbay Harbor Marina. The marina is in the heart of the waterfront and all the tourist destinations are an easy walk from the boat.

Boothbay is popular with summer visitors and it was exciting to see my book on display at Sherman's Book Shop. Two days was not adequate time for us to appreciate the many shops and restaurants in this charming tourist community.

Anne's Boat at Boothbay Harbor

4th Week of June

On Sunday afternoon we picked up a mooring at Billings Boatyard in Stonington on Deer Isle. It was foggy on Monday, so we used Anne's dinghy to go a short distance to the town dock. We had lobster rolls for lunch and held hands as we walked along the waterfront to visit a few shops and art galleries. I always enjoy visiting Stonington, a charming, picturesque lobster fishing community with traditional Downeast charm.

I wanted to enjoy our limited time together and did

not discuss the Jenkins case or the episode in the closet with Anne at anytime during our trip.

On Tuesday we returned to Stone Harbor and Anne immediately went to the Inn to catch up on business. Unfortunately, we were both preoccupied with pending work during much of our short time together. Once again, I was mostly a distraction after we returned to the Inn so I booked a flight to New York and returned my rental car in Portland on Wednesday.

20

When my flight landed at LaGuardia, I had a message from Mark on my cell phone; "Steve, if it's convenient, I would like to talk with you about the Jenkins case."

I returned his call; "I got your message. No problem, I just returned to New York. How about meeting tomorrow?"

Thursday afternoon I was in Mark's office:

"Steve, thanks for your help. Sorry about that incident in the closet. I am certainly glad you were unharmed. You seem to stumble into some dangerous situations. Please be careful."

"Now, let me get you up-to-date. Passport information indicated Jenkins departed to Nassau on a flight from Fort Lauderdale that same day. She departed Nassau the following day on a flight to London. She either switched passports or just boarded another flight and never entered England. They have no record of Pamala Jenkins going through customs and immigration."

"We suspect she has a significant amount of cash to pay her expenses so we are unlikely to trace her with credit card or cell phone activity. We don't know where she might be hiding."

"Now the interesting part. Jenkins has retained an attorney that has called our office in Palm Beach. He said his client was willing to cut a deal if we were interested. Our prosecutors told him we might be willing to talk if she is willing to tell us how to locate the money."

"That's when the story gets even more interesting. He said Jenkins is furious with McDonald who she says has the money. Jenkins claims she was just a front for McDonald and got deserted."

"As of now, we have no trace of McDonald. She wasn't our priority and we are not yet certain of her real identity. We are processing all the fingerprints at the office but have not isolated a set belonging to McDonald. She had her deserted apartment cleaned over that weekend so she was obviously alerted sometime before Saturday."

"At this time we suspect McDonald is an alias and she is traveling under another name. As you know, it's easier today than in the past to purchase a new identity on the Dark Web. Hackers post stolen health records, credit card information and passports for sale every day. The Dark Web is a virtual shopping mall for criminals."

"With our primary focus diverted to Jenkins it appears McDonald got a head start on everyone, including Jenkins."

"As a result, we have not been able to track the money or McDonald."

"Now I want to shift topics."

"Steve, our arrangement has worked exceptionally well on this case and I would like to make it an ongoing relationship. We both know and understand the parameters and limitations we need to respect. We worked on cases when you were at the bank for well over a decade and you can be a valuable asset to my team at this stage in your career."

"Mark, I retired so I could enjoy some non-bank activities and I am not interested in working full-time. I want to travel and enjoy my new boat."

"Steve, I understand your desire for independence and I am somewhat envious. I am not proposing a full-time relationship. I just want you to remain available as a consultant and I want to continue our professional arrangement with your firm, Paradox Research. Is that agreeable to you?"

I have always respected Mark's team and the work they do. It didn't take long for me to reply; "Yes, certainly."

Mark then surprised me; "Steve, you and Amanda work well together and your skills complement one another. I plan to assign the two of you to future cases but I ask this in return. You are not an employee and there is nothing to prevent a personal relationship between you and Amanda. I only ask that you tell me if you think anything in your relationship will have a negative impact on any investigation."

I was speechless for a moment; "Mark, you have caught me totally off-guard. I really admire Amanda but our relationship has always been completely professional. I can't imagine she would have any interest in a personal relationship with me."

"Steve, you might be surprised."

21

1st Week of July

After my meeting with Mark I returned to my co-op apartment in New York to spend the weekend and think about marketing my book. I was surprised by the number of business calls I was receiving. It was becoming apparent that I could make consulting a full-time activity. On the other hand, I can afford to be selective and only focus on assignments that are interesting. I needed to decide how busy I want to be and how I want to spend my time.

I grew restless after a few days in New York since most of my friends had gone out of the city to enjoy an extended 4th of July holiday. I returned to Palm Beach and Paradox on Sunday. I still considered New York my home but was spending less and less time in the city. Paradox gives me the freedom to move around and enjoy different locations but the boat is not a full-time alternative.

Tuesday morning I had another call from Mark.

"Steve, our prosecutors have been negotiating with Jenkins's attorney and have received a proposal I think we should consider. But we have a dilemma. We want to know what she has to say before we cut a deal and she wants a deal before she talks on the record."

"Her attorney has proposed on off-the-record meeting at a location out of the county. Jenkins is willing to share some information on the condition the information disclosed in that meeting not be used against her if we don't cut a deal. She is not willing to talk to an agent."

"We have agreed to her conditions subject to being able to use all the information we develop independently."

"Jenkins knows you and our attorney has explained you work as a consultant to the bank and are not an agent. After some back-and-forth negotiation, Jenkins has accepted you as her contact because she will recognize you."

I was uncertain how to respond. After a pause I asked;

"Mark, I'm not sure I want to do this. The last time I saw Jenkins she was damn angry and pointed a gun at me. What do you have in mind?"

Mark continued; "The plan is for you to fly to The

Bahamas and you will get further instructions after you arrive in Nassau. You will be met by her attorney and searched to make certain you do not have a phone or any recording device. Her attorney indicated he will then give you a new ticket to fly from Nassau to another country to meet with Jenkins. That's all I know."

"Mark, you got to be kidding me - right?"

"No, I am serious. We will have a small tracking device on you and you won't be alone. I plan to send Amanda along to follow you. Jenkins won't recognize Amanda and her attorney keeps referring to male agents in our negotiations. I don't think they will suspect a young woman traveling as a tourist."

"When am I supposed to fly to Nassau?"

"Thursday, after we get Amanda down to Florida."

Mark concluded; "Steve, pack for both cold and tropical weather. We don't have any idea where you might be going to meet Jenkins. Be careful, you can call this off at any time."

#   #   #

Thursday morning I boarded my flight to Nassau. When I had cleared customs a teenager with a hotel sign and my name approached me. He handed me an envelope, grabbed my bags and we headed for a taxi. He put my bags in the taxi and gave the driver directions to the hotel.

I opened the envelope before I got in the taxi and saw a hotel reservation in my name - nothing more.

My arrival at the hotel was uneventful. I showed my identification and was handed the key to a small suite on the fifth floor with a living area and bedroom overlooking the beach. When I looked around the living room, I saw an envelope addressed to me on the desk. Inside was a short message;

"Wait for instructions - don't leave this room - order room service."

About an hour after I arrived I heard a knock and looked through the eye-hole in the door. I recognized Jenkins's attorney from the briefing file I reviewed before departing to Nassau.

I admitted him and a second man into my room. The attorney said; "Please remain standing while my associate searches you and your room."

They departed about thirty minutes later satisfied I had followed instructions and had no cell phone or recording devices. I was very relieved they paid no attention to the luggage tags on my two small suitcases and my new wristwatch with the tracking chips enclosed.

I was feeling like a spy in a movie - the whole setup seemed unreal. I watched TV the rest of the day - bored and nervous at the same time. I received no further instructions and room service delivered dinner and breakfast the next morning.

At one o'clock on Friday I heard a knock on my door. The young room service delivery boy with my lunch was visible through the eye-hole and I opened the door. As the delivery boy was leaving, a tall blonde entered my room. She gave the delivery boy a big friendly smile, said; "thank you" and gave him a tip!

It took me a minute to recognize Jenkins as a fake blonde with big sunglasses and wearing a sexy tropical sundress. She looked like a typical tourist on vacation. Her friendly composure ended as the door closed and I was relieved she didn't pull a gun from her purse. She walked over to a chair, sat down and directed me to another chair. She stared at me with cold eyes and said;

"How the fuck did you figure out what was going on?"

I replied; "It's my job as a bank auditor. What do you want to tell me?"

She replied; "Just enough to get the FBI to negotiate a deal."

"OK, go ahead."

Jenkins was brief, bitter and to the point.

"I met the woman you call McDonald in Charlotte. She was a client assigned to me at the brokerage firm where I worked."

"One evening I invited her for drinks and I disclosed I had some financial troubles. I planned to ask if she could help and loan me some money. She was smooth and before I fully understood what was happening, we agreed to help one another and we moved to Palm Beach."

"She had some money from a prior scheme. It gave us the capital for me to look and act like a wealthy woman with an inheritance."

"Our deal was to split the money before we got caught and disappear to Europe to retire. She had already arranged for both of us to have new identities. It was going great. We thought we had another year or so - until you came along."

"She needed me to play the role of a debutante because she is short, overweight, dull looking with no social skills. She has no personality and couldn't pull it off without me."

"She did all the banking and that branch manager in Charlotte must have tipped her off. She cut out and left me. I didn't even know she was gone until that Monday morning - she just left a note on my desk telling me to avoid you and get out of town."

"That's when you walked in the office - I was so angry I could have shot you!"

"Now, her name is not McDonald and I know she has several fake identities and passports. You won't find her or the money without my help."

"She doubled crossed me and left without telling me - I am pissed and want her put in jail. I don't trust that woman. She scares the hell out of me."

"That's my story - tell the FBI to cut a deal and I will tell them how to find her and the money."

Jenkins stood up and walked out of the room. I hadn't said a word.

#   #   #

I stayed in the room for another hour to see if anything more was going to happen. When nothing did - no calls on the house phone and no visitors - I decided to check-out and booked the six o'clock flight back to Palm Beach.

When I approached the check-out desk I had to wait in line behind a very obnoxious tourist - the kind that gives traveling Americans a bad name. When I approached the counter I was informed everything was paid - no additional charges.

As I headed to the taxi stand about three o'clock, I saw Amanda standing near the elevator to observe my departure. She walked outside to light a cigarette, and I made certain she overheard my request for a taxi to the airport for my flight to Palm Beach.

I noticed Amanda arrive in the boarding area as I waited for my flight but she did not acknowledge me. I think my feelings were hurt when she also ignored me after our flight landed in Palm Beach.

#　　#　　#

Saturday morning I debriefed Amanda and the prosecutors about my meeting with Jenkins. They planned to meet with her attorney and negotiate a deal. We all wanted to find McDonald.

After the meeting ended, I asked; "Did you smoke that cigarette? Never saw you light up before."

"Absolutely not, just needed an excuse to follow you outside and find out where you were going. Put the damn thing out after you drove off in the taxi."

My cell phone rang as I was walking back to Paradox after our meeting. The call was from Amanda.

"Steve, we just learned Jenkins is dead. Room service found her body last night when they delivered her dinner at six o'clock."

"What the hell happened?"

"We don't know, her attorney said the initial police report says she was strangled, but it was not a sexual assault."

22

2nd Week of July

I couldn't understand what might have happened. Was it possible that McDonald had followed Jenkins?

Amanda had returned to Portland on Monday and I planned to hang around the marina for a few days. My spirits brightened when I spotted Ken Stewart walking down the dock at the marina.

"Ken, great to see you! What are you doing in Palm Beach?"

"We arrived last Friday. Had dinner with some friends we met a couple of years ago at Highbourne on Saturday and we plan to stay here most of the week."

"We like to use the boat every couple of weeks but we don't like to be in The Bahamas during hurricane season. So we visit marinas along the coast and this is one of our favorites."

"Why don't you come down to our boat this evening for drinks?"

"That sounds great, thank you."

# # #

Tuesday morning I received a call from an Attache' at the US Embassy in Nassau;

"Mr. Wilson, I need to inform you the Bahamian Police want to contact you and ask you some questions about a woman named Pamala Jenkins. We always encourage our citizens to cooperate but, depending on the circumstances, you may wish to retain an attorney."

I called Amanda to report the call and ask her advice.

Amanda brought me up-to-date; "Steve, this is what we know after talking with her attorney."

"As you know, her attorney was at the hotel in Nassau. He arranged the reservations and payments for the rooms. He was contacted by hotel management when the body was discovered to make the identification."

"He told us Jenkins was traveling under another name with a false passport that McDonald had provided her. She had a reservation to fly to

London later that night and catch a flight to Paris. Her attorney had made the hotel reservations for both you and Jenkins. The hotel provided records for the reservations he made to the Nassau Police. The Police contacted the Embassy to learn why there was a reservation in your name."

"Steve, we want to help them solve this murder but we don't want them involved in our investigation. You can discuss your response with one of our attorneys but you will need to retain a private attorney if you want representation."

"Be careful and good luck. You might be the last person to see Jenkins alive before she was killed some time between two and six o'clock."

#   #   #

Tuesday afternoon I was sitting in a conference room with an FBI attorney and a private criminal attorney Ken Stewart had suggested.

The FBI attorney opened the discussion; "Mr. Wilson, we want you to cooperate in their murder investigation but, as you know, we don't want the Nassau Police involved in our investigation."

"We suggest you call the Attache' and assure him you are willing to cooperate. Request the Police send you their questions in writing and you will in turn provide a written statement answering their questions. We don't want to establish a confrontational relationship that might happen if you had your attorney contact the Embassy and the Nassau Police."

Wednesday morning we were back in the conference room reviewing the questions the Nassau Police had provided to the Attache' at the Embassy. There were several pages of detailed background questions - they were asking my entire history from birth to today one question at a time.

The final page was an open-ended question asking:

"Why were you at the hotel meeting with a woman traveling with a false passport?"

After reviewing my answers with the attorneys, I provided the following brief handwritten response:

"I was only acquainted with the deceased as Pamala Jenkins and was not aware she was traveling with a false passport."

"As you know from my previous answers, I am a bank auditor retained by the bank in Palm Beach."

"Jenkins invited me to meet her in The Bahamas to discuss a discrepancy in one of her bank accounts. We met in my suite about one o'clock for about thirty minutes. It was a brief meeting. She provided me with the information I needed and she left my suite shortly after one-thirty."

"I checked out of the hotel about three o'clock and took a taxi to the airport to return to Florida on a six o'clock flight."

My attorney scanned the form with my handwritten answers and I emailed a copy to the Embassy that afternoon.

#   #   #

On Wednesday afternoon Ken spotted me on the docks; "Hey Steve, you seem busy for an old retired guy. Was that attorney helpful? What's up?"

"Thanks for asking. I have been working on a bank fraud case that got me locked in a closet at gunpoint a few weeks ago. Thanks for suggesting the attorney, he has been very helpful. Apparently I was the last person to visit with a woman killed in Nassau. The FBI has it under control and I hope to enjoy this nice weather for the next few days!"

"Why don't you join Frances and me tonight? We have a reservation at Pistache at seven-thirty. Let's walk up together."

"Ken, that sounds great. See you then."

It was a cool evening for August and we enjoyed our dinner at a table on the narrow outside porch. I was facing the entrance and shortly after we sat down I noticed two women leaving and one of them resembled the woman in the photo with Keith Jones.

We had an enjoyable evening with only a few questions from Frances about my visit with Anne in Maine. They shared highlights of their visit to Highbourne in early June. It was nice to be with them before they departed the marina on Thursday morning to return to their dock in Fort Lauderdale.

I was intrigued by my second sighting of the woman that resembled the person in the Yacht Club photos. I assumed she had stopped by Pistache with a friend after work for a drink at the bar. Maybe I should start having an evening drink at Pistache.

#   #   #

On Friday morning I received a call from Amanda; "Steve, I think we might be getting a break on finding McDonald. Jenkins's attorney suspects McDonald killed Jenkins to keep her from talking and has been sharing some information with our team."

"He was certain Jenkins had been in contact with McDonald. She called McDonald a greedy bitch, and that's when she told him to cut a deal."

"Jenkins disclosed a lot of information to him. He told us McDonald's name is Sally Campbell. He also provided us with the names on two fake US passports and a fake EU passport she has in her possession."

"Sally Campbell was convicted ten years ago for a minor bank fraud and served a year in prison. We have been able to track her movements for the past couple of years and suspect she has swindled a few other folks during her travels. The brokerage firm in Charlotte confirmed Jenkins was a broker and Sally McDonald was a client. So Jenkins's story checks."

"My case file still refers to her as McDonald. With this passport information we will locate her. I will keep you posted."

23

3rd Week of July

Mark had no additional assignments for me and Amanda was working in Portland. Anne was preoccupied with the Inn and any visit would most likely be an intrusion as it's the height of the tourist season in Maine. I had received no response from the Nassau Police.

I stayed on Paradox at the marina to work on a cybersecurity article requested by a national banking publication. I also had a couple of bank assignments that did not require travel.

The weather in Florida was hot and humid but so was New York. Early morning was still cool enough to ride my new bike along the bike path. There was a nice sea breeze at the dock and air conditioning for working onboard Paradox.

I justified my evening visits to the bar at Pistache as research to locate the mystery woman from the Yacht Club photo. No sign of her but the after work bar scene offered a humorous distraction.

Between five and six o'clock, a revolving group of professionally dressed mostly younger people would enter the restaurant and crowd around the small bar. There was lots of talk and flirting but I guess I didn't fit the profile to attract attention.

On Wednesday I got a call from Amanda; "McDonald was located in Croatia and has been apprehended. I will let you know when she is extradited to the States. It might be sooner rather than later. I suspect she might prefer one of our jails."

The weather had cooled a bit for July so I walked to E.R.Bradley's for dinner. This popular historic restaurant has dining on a covered porch with a casual open air atmosphere. I headed to the outdoor bar for a beer and to listen to the guitar player singing a Jimmy Buffett song. As I walked in I passed mystery woman with another woman as they were leaving the bar.

I took a chance and asked the bartender: "Was that Amanda Smith, she sure looked familiar."

"I have no idea. You need to ask her next time."

I was still not certain it was the same woman but my curiosity about those events at the Yacht Club troubled me.

4th Week of July

I was growing restless and a change of scenery would do me good. It was time for me to do a short offshore voyage alone to test my skills and I made a reservation at the Bahia Mar Marina in Fort Lauderdale.

After I arrived without incident on Monday, I gave Ken and Frances a call and invited them to dinner. They had hosted me on several occasions and it was time to reciprocate. Frances was out-of-town visiting her sister, but I made arrangements to meet Ken on Wednesday at the restaurant at Pier 66 that overlooks the Intracoastal Waterway.

Ken and I were smoking cigars on the outside deck after dinner when a rather short, rough looking man seemed to acknowledge Ken as he passed below us on the dock. The guy was still wearing sunglasses after sundown, was deeply tanned and had numerous tattoos on his well-muscled arms - I suspect he spent time in a gym. He was headed out of the marina wearing a colorful tropical shirt with jeans and boat shoes.

"Ken, I am curious, who was that fellow that just acknowledged you as he walked out of the marina?"

"Oh, that's Robert's boat captain. Robert frequently keeps his boat at this marina during hurricane season. He prefers to keep it at the Atlantis Marina over in Nassau most of the year. We met him at Highbourne several years ago and we run into him from time-to-time at a few of the marinas here in Florida and The Bahamas. Robert likes to spend time on his yacht."

"I think you will find it's a small world when it comes to boating in South Florida. You will get to know people that actually use their boats and you will meet all types of people on the docks."

Ken laughed and said; "Active boaters tend to be friendly and very casually dressed around the docks. You will find it's frequently difficult to tell if you are talking to a millionaire or a boat bum."

We continued smoking our cigars and enjoyed a quiet evening watching a few boats traveling along the Intracoastal. Ken turned to me and said;

"Steve, thanks for calling. I was looking forward to having dinner with you. It's the first time we have had a chance to talk without Anne or Frances sitting at the table."

"What can you tell me about your new business? How is it going?"

"Ken, the nature of my work means most of what I do remains confidential. What I can tell you is that I now work with a number of banks and the part I enjoy most is helping them investigate fraud. That was my specialty in New York and my experience can be very helpful to smaller banks."

"I am scheduling more meetings in September and October than I anticipated. I am not certain how much I still want to travel on business and many of these assignments require travel. My job in New York required me to travel frequently to our offices in the States and Europe. Unfortunately, I am accustomed to airline and airport food."

Ken then asked; "How do you like your boat? Is Paradox what you expected?"

"Probably better than I expected. I enjoy spending time on Paradox and find I am not returning to New York as frequently as I expected. I can't just live on the boat full-time. I have been a modern 'cliff dweller' and lived in high-rise buildings for over twenty years. Just not ready to think about more changes."

Ken responded; "I understand. We made a lot of changes when I sold the business and we moved to Fort Lauderdale. It took a while to get settled again."

"Don't worry, I won't ask about your relationship with Anne - I leave those conversations to Frances."

# # #

Amanda called with an update on Thursday; "Steve, we had a pre-extradition interview with McDonald in Croatia. She denies knowing anything about Jenkins's death and won't disclose the location of the money unless we cut a deal. Not a surprise, just wanted to let you know."

"How is it going in Palm Beach? Still enjoy being on Paradox?"

I answered; "Yes, the boat is great, but I wanted to test my navigation skills and did a short offshore voyage alone down to Fort Lauderdale. Everything went well - thanks for asking."

Amanda replied; "Well done. Have fun, I will keep you posted."

I returned to Palm Beach on Friday feeling good about my round-trip offshore voyage to Fort Lauderdale. I was also pleased my recent article had generated several potential new clients.

On the return voyage I had a call from Darcy asking if I could come by the bank in Palm Beach on Monday morning.

24

1st Week of August

I walked up to the bank on Monday morning and was greeted by a troubled bank president.

Darcy sighed; "Steve, Howard Adams is being a real pain in the ass. He blames the bank for not setting up a trust account and losing his money. He has threatened legal action, and I overheard him complaining about the bank at the club. He won't listen to me. Will you talk to him and explain what happened?"

"Darcy, I am not sure that's smart. I can't disclose anything about our investigation to Adams. Your best bet is to have the bank's attorney talk to him. Adams is probably creating some liability for himself."

"I know, that's what I thought, but our attorney won't talk to him unless Adams also has an attorney present. That just sounds like more trouble to me."

"I wanted to talk to you before taking any action. What a mess, the money is gone and Jenkins is dead. Now, Adams is telling stories about the bank. Very little about the bank was reported in newspaper articles describing the alleged Ponzi scheme until he started talking to anybody that would listen."

Just then we were interrupted by Darcy's assistant;

"Ms. Levin, Mr. Adams is in the bank and he demands to see you. He is being very loud and upsetting some of the staff and customers."

Darcy sighed again and looked at me; "See what I mean - please stay."

Darcy looked at her assistant; "Thanks, please show him in."

A minute later the assistant opened the door and Adams barged into Darcy's office.

Darcy acted calm and stood to meet him; "Good morning Howard, please have a seat. It's already hot today" and she handed him a glass of water.

Adams remained standing and in a boisterous voice; "Ms. Levin your bank owes me twenty-five million dollars - I got screwed because you didn't set up the proper trust account!"

I interrupted; "Mr. Adams that is not correct and you need to calm down until the facts are revealed in court."

"Who the hell are you to tell me to calm down!"

"I am the outside auditor that investigated this fraud."

Adams just gave me a look that could kill, sat down the water glass with a loud clunk and stormed out of Darcy's office.

Darcy breathed a sigh of relief and reached for the glass Adams had been holding.

"Stop, don't touch that glass again!"

She gave me a startled look; "Why not?"

"I want the FBI to get his fingerprints from that glass. You may need to have yours taken to confirm which prints belong to Adams."

"Why?"

"Please trust me for now."

# # #

I picked up the water glass with a paper towel, carefully put it in a plastic bag and took it to the

FBI office for examination. Once I delivered the glass, I called Amanda in Portland. When she answered I said; "Amanda, I think I might have met Jenkins's killer."

"What, how, where?"

"Let me back up first. When I was checking out of the Nassau hotel I had to wait behind an agitated and obnoxious American tourist. Well, I met him again in Darcy's office."

"Howard Adams and his wife were at the hotel that 4th of July week and he certainly had motive. He may have recognized Jenkins at some point and followed her to her room. I took a glass with some of his fingerprints to your Palm Beach office. Let's hope the Nassau Police checked for fingerprints at the crime scene - maybe we get a match."

"Well, I'll be damned."

Darcy visited the FBI office Tuesday morning and gave them a fresh set of her fingerprints. It was a clean glass, and we assumed the other fingerprints belonged to Adams.

To date, I had been the only contact with the Attache' at the Embassy so, once again, I was elected to make contact and send a copy of Adams's fingerprints by email with the following message;

"Please find attached a set of fingerprints that I respectfully ask you to forward to the investigator in charge of the Jenkins murder case. The inspector should contact me if he finds a match with fingerprints at the crime scene."

Thursday morning I received a call from a detective with the Nassau Police.

"Mr. Wilson, we have a match with those fingerprints. What do you know?"

I responded; "That's what I suspected. Please contact Amanda Smith at the FBI and she can discuss the case with you. Sorry, I am not authorized to say more."

2nd Week of August

Monday morning I met with Amanda at the FBI office in Palm Beach. She confirmed the FBI Crime Lab had validated a match with the fingerprints found at the crime scene and all the proper legal steps had been undertaken with The Bahamas to arrest Adams on suspicion of murder. The attorneys could then argue about his extradition to The Bahamas.

Amanda assembled a small team of agents and local police to make the arrest. She asked me to go with the team to identify Howard Adams.

Amanda was wearing a black jacket with big FBI letters on the front and back. She knocked on the front door to Adams's home at six o'clock on Monday evening. His wife answered the door;

"Hello, who are you and why are these police officers with you?"

"Mrs. Adams, I am Agent Amanda Smith with the FBI and I am here to talk to your husband, Howard Adams."

At that moment Adams appeared at the door and spotted me. He shouted; "You son of a bitch" and lunged in my direction.

I didn't see Amanda trip him but he landed face down on his front walk still swearing at me. Amanda quickly stepped forward and placed handcuffs on a now subdued Adams.

"Howard Adams, you are being placed under arrest at the request of the Bahamian authorities for the suspected murder of Pamala Jenkins."

The next sound was Mrs. Adams gasping and fainting.

Adams was read his rights and taken to the local jail. Amanda and I stayed with Mrs. Adams until a friend arrived to comfort her.

On the drive back to the office I turned to Amanda; "That was fast, did you trip him? If so, thank you, he is a big strong guy and could have done some serious damage to me."

She replied; "You know, we get training for such occasions but you seem to attract angry people. You need to be careful."

Amanda had an evening of paperwork and an early flight back to Portland on Tuesday. I certainly owed her a favor and missed having dinner with her.

25

I was happy to spend the balance of the week on Paradox preparing for my bank meetings in early September. I also undertook my new investigative activity each evening and alternated visiting the bars at both Pistache and Bradley's without spotting my mystery woman.

I was slowly adjusting to the Florida lifestyle. I generally wore one of the solid color boat shirts I had ordered with Paradox embroidered above the breast pocket. My gray trousers had been traded for khakis or jeans and my black Gucci dress shoes for Sperry boat shoes. I would still take along my new lightweight blue blazer on occasion if a restaurant was more formal. This was a major change from wearing suits and ties almost every day in New York.

On Thursday evening at Bradley's, a rather well endowed woman in a very low-cut colorful tropical sundress sat next to me at the bar. After ordering a glass of champagne she smiled and started a conversation.

"Hi, my name's Candy, what's yours?"

"Steve."

Candy asked; "What do you do for a living?"

I replied; "Retired bank auditor."

She replied; "That's nice."

That was clearly the wrong answer as she turned and started talking to the guy on the other side of her.

I thought my luck was changing on Friday evening when I walked into Bradley's. I spotted my mystery woman with her friend sitting at the bar - and there was an empty place next to her friend.

I approached and asked if the seat was taken. They were engaged in quiet conversation and just motioned OK. I ordered a Scotch and waited for an opportunity to start a conversation.

No luck, they both got up and walked out toward Clematis. Disappointed, I ordered another Scotch and fish sandwich at the bar. I was beginning to feel like a stalker.

3rd Week of August

I made another cybersecurity presentation at a

bank board retreat in Scottsdale, Arizona on Tuesday. Monday and Wednesday were both travel days with a change of aircraft in Dallas. The days were long, but I enjoyed the meeting with the board and the discussions with management. The good news was they wanted to retain me as a consultant - the bad news was the bank was located in Arizona. I liked the people and we signed a consulting agreement.

I was tired when I returned to Palm Beach late Wednesday but decided to relax and enjoy a nice dinner at Pistache after eating airport food during the week.

When I walked in, my mystery woman and her friend were sitting at the bar with an empty seat next to mystery woman. They had apparently just finished eating as the bartender was removing a couple of plates.

So I walked up and asked if the seat was taken and they gestured OK. I ordered my Scotch and waited for an opportunity to talk.

To my surprise, mystery woman turned my direction, smiled and asked; "What's a Paradox?"

I was confused for a moment but then replied; "Oh, you mean the name on my shirt. It's the name of my boat."

"That's interesting, why did you pick that name?"

"It's also the name of my company so it seemed to fit."

"Good idea. What do you do?"

I changed my story this time and answered; "Mostly retired and spend time cruising. How about you?"

"We are both attorneys."

I asked; "Do either of you spend time on boats?"

"Not really, but we occasionally get invited to go on a friend's yacht."

"Well my boat doesn't qualify as a yacht but I really enjoy cruising The Bahamas, especially the Exumas. I think the Staniel Cay Yacht Club is a fun place to visit. You ever been there?"

Mystery woman hesitated and then said; "No, doesn't sound familiar."

So I ventured a follow-up; "Funny, you sure look like a woman I saw at a party last November. I must be mistaken."

Mystery woman was now agitated; "Never been there, couldn't have been me. That's really an old over used pick up line - better luck next time."

With that, mystery woman turned to her friend; "Time to go."

She got up and headed out of the restaurant. Her friend looked a little confused and followed her out the door. I felt foolish I didn't ask their names. Stupid oversight on my part. I ordered another Scotch and went to a table for dinner.

At dinner I pulled out my cell phone and looked closely at the picture I had taken of the photo on the wall at the Yacht Club. Not a great photo but it looked like the same woman. Is that why she became upset and walked out - or was it just a bad pick up line?

26

4th Week of August

Ken and Frances arrived at Palm Harbor Marina on Monday to spend another week in Palm Beach. I looked forward to their visit as I enjoyed their company. They had been very helpful in introducing me to people in Florida's boating community. Ken was certainly right and people who use their boats tend to be very friendly.

For the next few days I skipped my nightly visits to the local bars to spot mystery woman and joined Ken for five o'clock cocktails on their boat. We discussed navigation systems, marinas, weather and all manner of nautical subjects. The more time I spent with Ken the more I learned.

On Wednesday evening a short, muscular man in a yacht captain's outfit looked our direction as he walked down the dock. As he passed, I said; "He looked familiar."

Ken replied; "Yes, that was Robert's captain. I think

we saw him on the docks one night at Pier 66."

"Right, guess I didn't recognize him in his captain's uniform. Is the boat in Palm Beach today?"

"It's down at the end of the dock. Robert comes up to meet with clients and he likes to stay on his boat rather than in a hotel. If he is in town, he might stop and say hello if he has time."

We returned to our discussion of the latest navigation software for our phones and computers. We were completely focused on a new iPad program when;

"Hey, Ken! Didn't know you were at this marina."

"Hello Robert. Just taking a break and we always enjoy a week in Palm Beach. You have time for a drink?"

"No sorry, not tonight. This is just a quick business trip and I fly back to Boston tomorrow night. Great to see you - say hi to Frances."

Robert started down the dock and I turned to Ken; "I know this sounds redundant but he also looked familiar, what does Robert do?"

"Robert is a lawyer from Maine and he has a very successful firm that negotiates large settlements for injured people - medical malpractice, auto defects, aircraft malfunction and other claims."

"Ken, was that Robert Alexander?"

"Yes, do you know the firm?"

"Not really, just came across the firm when I was doing some work for a bank in Maine. He looked familiar because I was introduced to him once by the bank's President as we were walking out of a restaurant."

Ken and I returned to our discussion about a new iPad navigation program. I departed a short time later for a social dinner with Darcy and her husband.

Ken invited me for cocktails again on Thursday but I suggested they come to Paradox for a change. Ken and Frances arrived as planned and I had wine and cheese set up on the back deck.

As they arrived Frances said; "Steve, I haven't been aboard until now. OK if I look around?"

"Absolutely, we all picked up a glass of wine and I must have shown them every nook and cranny of Paradox for the next hour. Active boaters like to look at and talk about boats. It was a delight to show them Paradox.

Ken was impressed with the technology setup on

my desk. "Steve, you have given me several ideas for our boat. I can see why you are so comfortable working from your boat. This setup is better than my office at home."

After the boat tour Frances said; "Let's go get a pizza."

We walked to a small cafe near Clematis and ordered pizza. We crowded around a cozy outside table with a glass of wine.

Frances looked at me and said; "Tell me about you and Anne."

I looked back at Frances; "Wow, I wasn't expecting that - what do you want to know?"

"I have known Anne for a long time and she is one of my best friends. I also know she has to keep busy. I was grateful you wanted to buy a boat - she was getting bored and restless - it gave her a project during her visit with us."

I replied; "Yes, I know, we both need to keep busy. I am still trying to figure out this retirement thing."

Frances resumed; "I understand, I wondered how her husband's retirement plans would work out when they moved to Maine. He was ready to relax and Anne still needed projects. I assume you know Anne purchased both the boat and the Inn."

I responded; "Frances, Anne and I are still just getting to know one another. We had a rather awkward start last year but we seem to enjoy being together, especially on the boat."

Frances inquired; "Why are you still in Palm Beach? You are missing a glorious summer in Maine."

"Frances, we had a great trip together on her boat in June but the Inn becomes a full-time job the rest of the summer. I was a distraction after we returned to Stone Harbor in June. Work always came first for me so I understand Anne's priorities."

Thankfully, the pizza arrived and we could switch back to talking about activities around the Clematis neighborhood. I wondered if Frances had the same conversation with Anne.

The Stewarts had a dinner engagement with some friends in Palm Beach on Friday evening and I took a walk along the waterfront with plans to have a hamburger at a cafe on Clematis. My quiet walk was abruptly interrupted by an ambulance and several police cars with lights flashing. I stopped to join the assembled onlookers at what appeared to be a crime scene in front of a high-rise apartment building. I asked; "What's happening?"

"Some woman either jumped or fell from that building a short while ago."

That's more than I wanted to know and walked on to Clematis and my hamburger. I never know how to react to a tragedy - it just makes me sad.

Ken and Frances departed the marina at sunrise on Saturday and I only had time to wave before they crossed under the Flagler Memorial Bridge and headed north toward the inlet for their return voyage to Fort Lauderdale.

27

1st Week of September - Labor Day

Monday was Labor Day, and the airport was extra busy on Tuesday morning when I arrived for my morning flight to Denver. I made another cybersecurity presentation to a bank board on Wednesday with a return through Charlotte to make a similar presentation for a regional meeting of community bank auditors on Thursday.

I enjoyed my new consulting business, but I was not excited about spending this much time on airplanes. I was ready to be back in Palm Beach on Paradox for the weekend.

2nd Week of September

Amanda called on Monday; "McDonald has waived extradition and will be returned to Palm Beach in a few days. She revealed the location of about fifty million dollars and said she will provide an accounting to validate that is all that remains. She wanted out of that jail in Croatia. Our attorneys didn't need to make any type of deal."

"You won't be surprised to hear McDonald now claims Jenkins was the mastermind. She claims she was just following instructions and holding the money for safekeeping. The documentation and testimony you will be providing in court will certainly contradict her story."

"We also have a statement from the bank branch manager in Charlotte. He admitted he called McDonald when the bank's audit department asked him about the transfers to Switzerland. It appears to have been an innocent call, and they have found no evidence he knew about the scam."

I reflected; "If that much money remains then the investors should recover about half of the money they invested in her fake investment fund."

I said; "Think about it, Adams's wife will still have at least twelve million dollars and her hot-headed husband will be in jail over in The Bahamas for murder. You can't just make this stuff up - reality is stranger than fiction."

Amanda added; "Steve, one more thing. Mark has me doing a bank fraud investigation in Miami. It looks like a simple loan fraud where a real estate investor sold an office building but didn't repay the bank loan as required. He tried to disappear with about five million dollars but didn't get far. Mark said it's a clear cut case and there is no need for you to help with the investigation."

"I understand, you will do just fine."

"I am not asking you to help. I am hoping we can find time to have dinner one night later this week while I am in Florida. Will that work for you?"

"Certainly, I can take the new train down to Miami whenever it's most convenient for you. I don't have travel plans this week for a change."

"Let's plan on Wednesday night. I will make reservations."

The new intercity train was fast with only one stop in Fort Lauderdale. The tracks are all street level passing through densely populated communities - not elevated like Chicago or underground like the New York subway system. I suspect the drivers I saw waiting at the railroad crossings were not pleased with the traffic delays created by this new fast passenger train and the slow freight trains we passed on my ride to Miami.

The auto dealer case at the bank in Portland had been assigned to Amanda. She updated me on her investigation at dinner.

"Steve, you know it's sad people do such stupid things when it comes to money."

"That restaurant owner had diverted less than one hundred thousand dollars into the auto purchase scheme. At the most it might have saved him about thirty thousand dollars in taxes but it will cost him dearly with back-taxes, fines and possible jail time."

"The auto dealer only made a few thousand dollars and he ends up charged with being an accomplice to tax fraud. Not certain what will happen with him."

"It seems they were friends and cooked up this silly scheme over beers at a local bar. 'Everybody does it' was their only defense."

"Tory did a thorough job with her investigation and it made my job easy. Thank you."

Amanda concluded; "I know it's our job to find the bad guys, but it seems we uncover a lot of stupidity."

I had to agree; "That's true in so many cases, but we do locate and help stop a lot of career criminal activity. I find helping stop drug dealers and con artists like McDonald rewarding. Their crimes hurt innocent families."

"I learned while at the bank in New York that South Florida is a hot bed for con artist activity. I guess they like the warm weather and Florida is fertile ground for a scam. Naive, retired people looking for higher investment returns must look like easy targets. McDonald is not a unique case."

I was glad Amanda called me but our conversation was mostly business or casual discussion about all the new buildings and restaurants in Miami. After dinner, I took the late train back to Palm Beach.

Amanda returned to Portland the following day.

28

On Thursday I got a call from a senior federal banking regulator I knew from my banking days.

"Steve, we have a bank headquartered in Miami that has been ignoring the cybersecurity recommendations our examiner made after we discovered a computer intrusion last year. In fact, this is not the only repeat recommendation they have been ignoring. We just completed a meeting to discuss the situation. I have concluded the bank's board and management have a systemic financial controls problem."

"We have notified Mrs. Martinez, the bank's Board Chair, that we are requiring the board hire a consultant to conduct what we call a Management Study. We designate an independent board member as the point person for such studies. The Board Chair is that contact, and she has asked our examiner for the names of consultants we could approve for the study."

"Our initial focus is their failure to adopt our

cybersecurity recommendations and your firm is a perfect fit. I want to let you know I added your name to the list of consultants we could approve."

Friday morning I received a call from the bank's Board Chair asking if I would submit a proposal. She emailed the regulatory order to me, and I prepared a short proposal. I submitted it to her by email Sunday evening.

3rd Week of September

I received a call on Monday from the Board Chair and she requested a meeting at the bank's offices in Miami the next morning. She was brief and to the point at our meeting;

"Our President wants to get this over with so we can move on to more important business. Just tell us what we need to do to make the regulators happy. Our President says that examiner is just being a pain to our management team."

I explained; "Like I outlined in my proposal, I need to follow the requirements of the regulatory order if you are going to resolve this issue. Most important, I will need to conduct private interviews with all eight of your board members and at least six of the bank's executive officers."

"Is it necessary to talk to everyone? That seems an unnecessary diversion of all our time. We are all busy people. The President says he can answer all your questions."

"Yes, it's necessary for me to talk to everyone."

On Wednesday I had scheduled a meeting with another bank's management team to discuss risk management. Fortunately, the bank had a video conference room and I could participate from my desk on Paradox. The video process worked better than I expected and I hoped such a system might help cut down on some future travel.

The Board Chair at the bank in Miami had directed the board secretary to arrange private meetings with both board members and management for Thursday and Friday. She said the President was in a hurry to get the study concluded and they had booked a full schedule of seven interviews each day for me.

I didn't know what I expected to find. I was not permitted by bank regulations to read the confidential Report of Examination so I didn't know what concerns the regulators had expressed. My report was to be an independent evaluation.

I had learned as an auditor that people will say the most extraordinary things if you just let them talk. Asking questions and taking notes makes people nervous. I do ask a question to start a conversation, but if I keep my mouth shut after the first answer most people can't seem to stand a brief silence and they start talking again.

I simply began each interview with the same brief description of the study and asked;

"Please describe how the board provides oversight of the bank's cybersecurity program?"

The answers from board members were consistent:

"That's not our job, we rely on our President."

"Our President told us there was no intrusion and the regulators are wrong. He told us we have an incompetent bank examiner and these regulations are nonsense."

"Our President says our internal auditor has confirmed that we are fully protected and we have no cybersecurity risk."

"Our President says our auditor has confirmed all our financial controls are air-tight and we have no risk of fraud or embezzlement."

"I don't understand why the examiner was concerned about our President's expense account. He needs to entertain our clients."

The bank's Executive Officers all said; "Our President is a member of the board and he provides the board with all the required reports."

I had reviewed the last two internal audit reports the President had submitted to the board before I started my interviews. The President's audit reports to the board were basically useless as they contained no detailed information about the bank's cybersecurity protections.

The attitude of the President and his four senior officers was consistent with the statements from his board members. It was clear this executive management team had no respect for board oversight, bank examiners or bank regulation.

My final interview was with the bank's young auditor and I took the same informal approach.

The auditor was nervous and was obviously afraid he would be blamed for any examination problems. The President had assigned responsibility for compliance with past regulatory orders to the bank's auditor. The President had mentioned to me he was worried about the auditor's work in our interview and he blamed the young auditor for the bank's current regulatory problems.

I wasn't learning much from the auditor until he finally blurted out;

"You don't understand! I submit all my reports to the board audit committee. Our President is a member of the committee. I never have a private session with our independent directors. He edits all my reports before I present them to the committee. It's his rule, 'no bad news' is to be presented to the audit committee or the board of directors."

I then asked; "Why did the regulators question your audit of the President's expense account?"

"What audit? I am not allowed to even look at any of the executive officers' expense accounts or their loans with the bank. I never wrote an audit report about his expenses and the President has never given me a copy of the bank's examination reports. He just tells me what to put in my responses."

"Mr. Wilson, I know this isn't right. That's why I am looking for a new job."

I had a brief exit meeting with the Board Chair and President late Friday before I headed back to Palm Beach on the train. I reported;

"Thanks for arranging all my meetings and being so cooperative. This should conclude the interview process. As required by the order I will come back Monday to review some of the bank's operations and computer systems. That should only take one day and I should have my report completed on Wednesday."

The President responded; "Thanks, we appreciate your help in so quickly getting bank regulators off our back. I assume we will see a draft copy of your report and I can make any needed corrections before you send it to the regulators."

My only response was; "I will be at the bank at eight o'clock on Monday and hope to finish my systems review in one day. Thanks again for your cooperation."

I wrote notes about each interview on the return train ride to Palm Beach. I spent most of the weekend compiling my thoughts and preparing a draft outline for my report.

On Saturday night I walked up to an outdoor cafe on Clematis for a sandwich. I was preoccupied thinking about my report when I noticed a woman stop for a minute to look at me. She had resumed her walk before I recognized her as the mystery woman's friend. I assumed she noticed I was wearing the same bright blue Paradox boat shirt I had been wearing at the Pistache bar.

29

4th Week of September

I arrived at the bank in Miami at eight o'clock
Monday morning and was led by the bank's young
auditor to an empty office with a computer on the
desk. He put in the required passcodes and I was
given read-only access to the operating and
financial systems I needed to examine.

Most smaller community banks utilize software
systems provided by independent vendors. I was
relieved to find the bank in Miami used the same
systems as the bank in Palm Beach. As a result, I
had no learning curve.

I was shocked to find the bank had purchased no
extra security software to protect customer
accounts from hackers. In addition, many of the
normal financial checks-and-balances were not
incorporated with the bank's internal accounting
systems. The lack of these financial controls made
my review easier as there were few control
systems to evaluate.

I checked all the executive officers' loan accounts and although they were on very favorable terms they appeared to be in order.

When I checked the bank's account payables, I discovered inadequate approval systems for payment of expenses. Both the President and Chief Financial Officer had authority to pay their own credit card charges and they could pay any vender invoice with just one signature. No confirmation of the expense was required before a bank clerk made payment.

I reviewed the records for both the President's and the Chief Financial Officer's expense accounts and understood the regulatory concerns. Both made liberal use of a bank credit card and many of the expenses looked personal in nature.

As a result, I examined payments to vendors approved by these two officers in more detail.

Again, many of the payments authorized by both the President and Chief Financial Officer appeared to be personal in nature. I made note of several unusual items purchased by the bank for both their homes.

The Chief Financial Officer appeared to approve nearly all business-related expenses with no independent review. I was not surprised to see a pattern of recurring payments made for rent, utilities and other regular monthly expenses. However, I decided to test a few of the other recurring payments I didn't fully understand. One such expense was for equipment maintenance provided by a local firm. Out of curiosity I opened my laptop and did an internet search and found no such firm listed in Miami or Fort Lauderdale.

The next step was to check state records for any business registration - no such firm. The monthly payments were all made to a post office box in Fort Lauderdale. The monthly invoice contained no phone number for the company and the post office box was the only address listed.

The financial records indicated a check was automatically mailed to the post office box each month. My next step was to look at the bank's checking account and examine images of the checks deposited by the firm in question.

I am not a handwriting expert, but the signature on the back of each check's image certainly resembled the handwriting of the Chief Financial Officer. A little further investigation indicated monthly payments of thirty thousand dollars to this firm had started three years ago - a total of one million dollars had been disbursed.

I wasn't certain how I was expected to proceed. I was not hired by the board to do an audit. Technically, the board had hired me to submit a report to bank regulators. This regulatory investigation and report was new territory for me and I needed to plan my approach.

At the end of the day, I called the Board Chair and requested a private session with her on Wednesday morning before the two of us were scheduled to meet with the President at lunch to discuss my report.

#   #   #

Wednesday morning I met with Mrs. Martinez, the Board Chair, in her office at a prominent charitable organization to insure privacy.

"You and the other independent board members are all respected members of Miami's business community. My research indicates your reputations are first rate and I suspect that's why the President recruited each of you to join the bank's board."

"I have discovered some significant problems at your bank and I want to share my findings and recommendations with you before I make my presentation to your full board tomorrow."

"First, the primary assignment was to evaluate the bank's cybersecurity systems. Frankly, there are no significant systems to evaluate and the bank is very vulnerable to hackers. The cybersecurity reports your President has presented to your board are falsified - they are not the same reports prepared by your internal auditor."

She remained silent with a pensive frown.

"Second, as you will recall, the regulatory order also required an independent evaluation of the bank's financial systems and internal controls. This is an area of major concern. Let me ask you some questions."

"Did you or the board know the bank purchased a vacation home for the bank's President in The Bahamas?"

The Board Chair was startled; "No, are you sure?"

"Did you know the bank has purchased over one hundred thousand dollars of artwork and other items for your President's personal residence?"

An increasingly concerned Chair responded; "The President never discussed such purchases with our board. Are you certain?"

I added; "Yes, I have attached copies of the invoices and delivery instructions to my report."

"Now, I want to shift our discussion to my findings related to your Chief Financial Officer."

"Did you or the board know the bank has purchased about thirty thousand dollars of furnishings for his personal residence?"

"No" answered a very unhappy Board Chair.

"The next topic is the most difficult part of our discussion this morning. I have found evidence of a possible embezzlement."

"Oh my God - what next?"

"My recommendation is that you contact the bank's internal auditor and ask him to conduct an examination of the accounts in question. Based on my interview, I believe he is fully capable of providing your independent board members with the information you will require concerning this matter."

"To protect your reputations, it is best the board take full control of this investigation. You will want to contact an independent attorney to counsel your board. I don't think it's advisable for you to use the bank's attorney as he was retained by your President - but that is your decision."

"My recommendation is the board place both the President and the Chief Financial Officer on a leave of absence until the facts are known. They should not be informed of my recommendation prior to my presentation to your board meeting tomorrow."

"What do we tell the President today? We are

supposed to have lunch with him to discuss your report."

"You may call him and tell him I have told you my report is directed to the full board of directors and it is inappropriate for management to review the report in advance. I suggest you also tell him you have a business conflict today for lunch and will see him at the board meeting tomorrow."

"Finally, you should direct me to share my findings with the bank's internal auditor today."

"Mr. Wilson, I am in shock. Is it OK if I share this conversation with other directors?"

"You may do as you wish but I suggest you make certain they understand this information is not to be shared with the President or Chief Financial Officer prior to tomorrow's board meeting."

"OK, understood. Let's call the internal auditor, I want to get to the bottom of this as quickly as possible."

#   #   #

I wanted to avoid any pre-meeting discussion and walked into the bank on Thursday morning just a few minutes before the board meeting was scheduled to start.

The President was clearly angry with me when he

announced he was ready to start the meeting. I assumed from his actions that he typically ran the board meetings rather than the Board Chair.

I was pleased to see the Board Chair take control.

"Thank you, but I will run today's meeting."

"We are meeting today to receive the report Mr. Wilson will submit to bank regulators later today. I want each of you to know Mr. Wilson shared his findings with me yesterday. I have also asked the Chief Financial Officer to join our meeting today due to the nature of the report."

The President interrupted; "I have not had an opportunity to review that report and correct any errors! This is unacceptable!"

The Board Chair continued; "Mr. President, you may raise any objections once the report is presented. I fully intend to give you that opportunity. Mr. Wilson, please proceed."

My presentation was very detailed and my findings were fully documented in the exhibits. The President and Chief Financial Officer both stood up and walked out of the meeting following my disclosure of the bank's purchase of the President's vacation home in The Bahamas and the personal items purchased for each of their homes.

The directors asked numerous detailed questions and the meeting continued for another two hours before I concluded.

At the conclusion of the meeting, the board voted to place the President and Chief Financial Officer on a leave of absence pending the outcome of the internal auditor's report. The Board Chair was designated as acting Chief Executive Officer.

#   #   #

The Board Chair asked that I remain at the bank after the meeting and provide recommendations concerning her next steps. As I suspected from our interview, Mrs. Martinez was an experienced executive and she didn't need much advice.

Her meeting after the board meeting with the young internal auditor was brief and to the point. She disclosed the board's actions to the auditor and asked him to document all the facts as quickly as possible. She assured the auditor he had the full support of the board.

The board submitted my report to the bank's regulators that afternoon, and I took the evening train back to Palm Beach. I expected the regulators would promptly contact the FBI.

It had been a busy week. My simple assignment had uncovered a can of worms. I did not find this type of assignment enjoyable and was not certain I would volunteer to do another Management Study for bank regulators.

I expect both the President and Chief Financial Officer will face legal action by federal authorities. It's unfortunate the media's focus on negative actions by a few people harms the image of the entire banking industry. My experience as an auditor indicates the overwhelming majority of bankers exhibit high integrity and are dedicated to providing professional service for their customers.

#　　#　　#

On Saturday I called Anne rather than text or email as we hadn't spoken much since our boat voyage in June. We had a brief conversation about the weather but a guest at her Inn interrupted. Our call was too short to share any real news.

30

1st Week of October

Mark called me Tuesday morning to report the bank's regulators had notified the FBI about the suspected fraud at the bank in Miami. He said he was not surprised when my name surfaced as the author of the Management Study.

He told me his South Florida agents were still engaged in a significant money laundering investigation related to one of the international drug cartels. As a result, he was planning to assign Amanda to the bank investigation as she was already known to the South Florida team.

I was disappointed when Mark said; "Steve, I assume your report is fully documented. I see no need to retain you as a consultant on the case. Amanda can handle it."

#   #   #

Tuesday afternoon I received a call from Ken

Stewart; "Steve, we plan to take the boat down to Miami tomorrow. I don't think you have spent any time along the Miami waterfront so why don't you take that boat of yours south and join us for a few days?"

Later than night I sent a text to Anne telling her I was planning to take Paradox to Miami and spend a few days with Ken and Frances. She responded the next morning; "Have fun, they are nice people."

The weather was agreeable on Thursday with a light wind from the southeast and a light chop on the ocean. It was an ideal day to take Paradox offshore alone and navigate the sixty nautical miles from Palm Beach to Government Cut and the Port of Miami. As I entered the port I cruised by several container ships, passed the downtown Miami skyline and arrived late afternoon at Dinner Key Marina in Coconut Grove.

Ken and Frances greeted me when I arrived at the marina. We walked over to Monty's Coconut Grove waterfront restaurant for dinner that evening to celebrate my offshore passage.

I assumed Amanda was working with the bank auditor to document the case for the federal prosecutors. I sent her a text Friday afternoon to tell her I had been invited to bring Paradox down to Miami and join friends at the marina.

190

Amanda called me Saturday morning. "Steve, what a nice surprise. I have plans with friends this weekend but would love to meet you for dinner Sunday Night. I will make a reservation."

"That sounds great - see you Sunday."

I took a long walk along the Coconut Grove waterfront that morning and returned in time to join Ken and Frances on their boat for lunch. When I arrived, Ken was busy reviewing documents on the back deck and was deep in thought.

"Hey Ken, am I interrupting?"

"Not at all, please come aboard. We are expecting you for lunch. Did you enjoy your walk?"

"It was very nice - I like to explore and walk a mile or more every day for fresh air and exercise. I don't always have access to a gym."

"Sorry to interrupt. It looked like you were deep in thought."

Ken replied; "No problem, I was just thinking about a potential investment. I don't like tying up funds in private placements but my existing investment has performed as advertised."

As Ken picked up the folder I couldn't help but notice the name on the file: Alexander Law Firm.

I hesitated but then asked; "Ken, I don't mean to pry but is that the Alexander firm in Portland?"

"That's right, you might recall we said hello to Robert on the docks in Palm Beach. We met him about four years ago on our first long stay at Highbourne. He was there for a few days on his boat."

At that point Frances served lunch and our conversation focused on what I had seen in Miami on my morning walk.

After lunch Ken asked; "Did you ever audit private placements?"

"Sometimes, but that wasn't the focus of my job at the bank. Today I don't have sufficient net worth to commit any funds to a private placement with a hedge fund or a private equity firm."

Ken replied; "Good judgement. I have the net worth but I want to keep it so I try to avoid too much risk."

"I already have three million dollars invested with Robert so I think I will pass on this insurance settlement."

"Is it OK if I ask how something like that works?"

"Sure, no problem. Robert's firm has a great track

record in certain types of damage litigation. They represent people or businesses that have been seriously damaged in some manner. My existing investment was a medical malpractice settlement."

"The insurance company for the hospital agreed to a large confidential settlement to be paid over time. The insurance companies don't want these large amounts to be public because they fear it will just attract more litigation. In this case, the people who were harmed wanted the money up front, not over time."

"So Robert arranged for a group of investors, including me, to pay those people a certain amount of cash up front and in return they assigned all future payments from the insurance company to the investment group. We receive quarterly payments and our rate of return is about ten percent. That's a better-than-average return but our money is received over time and we have no liquidity."

I asked; "So the money you receive is actually from the insurance company. That sounds pretty safe. What's the name of the company?"

Ken replied; "I don't know, the settlement was confidential and everyone involved in the settlement signed a non-disclosure agreement."

I consider such confidentially to be a 'red flag'. I

didn't want to alarm Ken, so I asked; "If the payments don't come directly from the insurance company - who does issue the check?"

Ken replied; "The check originally came from a bank in Portland but Robert changed banks early this year and they now come from a bank in Boston."

At that point Frances came out to join us and said;

"I want to do some shopping and Ken needs to get off this boat and get some exercise. Would you like to join us?"

"No thanks, I enjoyed lunch, thanks for the invitation. See you later."

31

2nd Week of October

Amanda made dinner reservations for 7:30 on Sunday evening at an up-scale restaurant on top of one of the new downtown buildings. I took a taxi to the building and stepped on the high-speed elevator up to the restaurant to wait for Amanda. I arrived about fifteen minutes early and, as I expected, she stepped off the elevator promptly at 7:30.

Amanda looked very elegant with her hair up. She was wearing a conservative light blue pantsuit with a yellow blouse and dark blue scarf. She carried her small, black leather backpack as her purse. We were seated promptly at a window table with a magnificent view of Biscayne Bay.

"Steve, great to see you, I don't want to talk business tonight but I want to thank you for doing such a thorough job of documentation. The more we dig, the more we find. I hope to turn the case over to the prosecutors by the end of the week."

"Now, tell me about your voyage down the coast. It sounds like you are becoming very comfortable on Paradox."

We had another memorable seafood meal and enjoyable conversation about boats and South Florida. We had a brief discussion about the check but Amanda agreed I could pay if she could pay next time. I thought it was time to stop splitting the bill as we had done in the past. We both avoided anything too personal until we were about to leave and Amanda asked;

"Steve, when was the last time you were in New York for any length of time?"

I had to stop and think; "I guess it might have been last June or July when I was there for several days. I find Paradox to be surprisingly comfortable and it's easy to work from the boat. Strange, I haven't thought much about it."

Amanda replied; "I get to the city from time-to-time for meetings with Mark and some of the team. Let's arrange to cross paths, I would love to see the city with someone that knows their way around."

After dinner, Amanda requested an Uber on her phone and I took a taxi back to the boat.

#   #   #

My curiosity about the law firm's clearing accounts at the Rockland branch was now on high alert. The similarity between the law firm's clearing accounts and those established by Jenkins and McDonald was frightening.

I was on retainer as a risk consultant to the bank in Maine and Tory would occasionally call me with questions. It was my turn to ask Tory a question. I called her Monday morning to ask about the law firm's clearing accounts.

"Tory, do you recall our discussion about those accounts in Rockland that Alexander's law firm had opened?"

"Certainly."

"As I recall, you said the accounts had been closed and moved to another bank. Correct?"

"Yes, that's right."

"Can you still access transactions in those closed accounts and see if any of the checks were written to a Ken Stewart?"

"If you find the account, I would like to know the source of the funds deposited into that account."

"Sure, it shouldn't take too long. Can I call you back?"

"Sure, anytime. Thank you."

A short while later Tory called me.

"Steve, I located the account in question. It was one of the accounts at the Rockland branch. Quarterly distributions were made to a Kenneth Stewart in Fort Lauderdale. Distributions were also made to five other individuals. Shortly before the distributions were made, a wire transfer was received from a large insurance company headquartered in New York."

"What more do you want to know?"

"Tory, thank you for confirming those transactions. Everything is in order and that's all I needed to know."

My curiosity frequently leads me down a blind alley. I was relieved Ken's account with Alexander was as advertised and all the transactions were legitimate.

32

Florida's weather looked good for the next few days but I was concerned about a storm moving across the country. I had a business trip planned on Thursday, so it was time to take Paradox back to Palm Beach. I relished a quiet day at sea as the sounds of Miami faded behind Paradox.

I don't trust early morning flights to arrive on time for important meetings, so I plan arrive the night before to avoid delays and rescheduling. I arrived at Reagan Airport on Wednesday night for a meeting to discuss cybersecurity risk with bank regulators in Washington.

This was my first such meeting to discuss regulatory strategy rather than a specific case. I was impressed with the caliber of people in our meeting; they were all very knowledgeable and completely focused on protecting bank customers.

I continued on to New York to spend a few days in the city after my meeting in Washington. Most of my friends in the city are business related and everyone works long hours. I reconnected with a banker friend for lunch on Friday and a bond trader for lunch on Saturday. I enjoyed jazz at Lincoln Center Saturday evening with a couple of attorneys that worked at the bank. I joined a couple that lived in my building for brunch at a neighborhood cafe on Sunday. It was a great visit but everyone was busy again with work starting Monday.

I was beginning to understand why retirement can be so difficult if you don't have something to do after you stop going to the office every day. I had always worked long hours, frequently ate dinner at neighborhood restaurants and my apartment was mostly for watching the news, an occasional movie and sleeping. I was feeling out of place being back in the city now that my book was published.

I had to smile when I looked in my closet Saturday morning. I was looking for something casual to wear and realized I had accumulated several dozen business suits and even more dress shirts. I was afraid to count the number of ties I owned.

I had another small closet dedicated mostly to the cold weather clothing and boots I had purchased last year in Maine. I had no reason to take these items to Florida.

I had three suits, six dress shirts and a dozen ties on Paradox for business meetings with bankers. These business suits got the most use when I traveled to make presentations. I realized on a day-to-day basis I had completely shifted to Florida's more relaxed life-style.

Being on Paradox at a marina provided lots of activity and most people were friendly. My technology setup on Paradox was much better than using my laptop at my apartment in New York. I could duplicate the setup at my apartment, but it was becoming clear I preferred to be in Florida on Paradox.

I didn't want to think about moving from New York, the city has been my home for over fifteen years.

3rd Week of October

I had another video conference on Wednesday afternoon and returned to Palm Beach on Monday evening. I prefer to do these video conferences using the technology available on the boat.

Wednesday night I was sitting outside at a restaurant on Clematis having a beer and hamburger when mystery woman's friend walked past. My earlier attention had been focused on the mystery woman but I now recognized her friend. I was surprised when she turned around and came back and stood next to my table.

"Aren't you the fellow that asked Donna if she had been in The Bahamas last year?"

I stood up to be polite; "Yes, I thought she looked familiar but as I recall, she thought it was a bad pick up line."

"Well, she got really irritated by your question."

I replied; "Sorry, tell her I apologize. I was just trying to be friendly."

As she turned and walked away, she said; "I wish I could tell her - it's too late - she's dead."

33

I was stunned and remained standing for a while and finally sat back down, reflecting on what just happened. What was that about?

I finished my burger and ordered another beer and pondered our brief encounter. I still knew nothing about this mystery woman or the woman who stopped by my table.

Mystery woman's name was Donna and my mention of the party at the Yacht Club had upset her. Was it a bad pick up line or had I hit a nerve? I was now even more curious; who was she and when did she die?

On Thursday morning I started a search of Palm Beach obituaries for a woman named Donna. I located several but none of the photos resembled the mystery woman.

I had to assume she worked in Palm Beach but her friend didn't say how, when or where she had died. Her obituary might have been published in her hometown newspaper. I was stumped for now.

After lunch on the boat I shifted my focus. If they were both attorneys, then they must work at a nearby office. I didn't know if they worked at the same firm or were just friends. However, most law firms have pictures of their attorneys on their websites. Maybe I could locate their photos online.

It was a tedious task to systematically search the internet for the address of each nearby law office and to review the photos on their websites. By the end of the afternoon I was ready to take a walk and get a beer. My eyes hurt and I had been unsuccessful in locating a photo of either woman.

#   #   #

I was tired after doing boat projects on Saturday and walked to Bradley's that evening for a beer and a shrimp basket. When I walked in I spotted Donna's friend at the bar with another woman. It was busy and there were no empty seats but I walked up and said; "Hello".

She turned and gave me a cold stare; "Who are you?"

I decided to be completely open; "My name is Steve Wilson, this is my card."

As she took my card I asked; "Can we exchange?"

I received an abrupt; "No!" She stood up and walked out followed by a confused friend.

I stood there suffering the sorry looks of the people at the bar that had witnessed the exchange. I was embarrassed and asked for a table rather than have my first beer at the bar.

34

4th Week of October

My meeting Monday was a video call with my client in Arizona. I was pleased with how well this technology worked with established clients. However, I did not find it effective for initial meetings with new clients or board presentations. I was finding a video conference is great for sharing information but it does not let me get the feeling of the meeting by observing the reactions of individual participants. I find complex business discussions required in-person meetings. It was apparent I would keep my priority status this year as a frequent flyer.

Late Monday I got a call from the head prosecutor for the McDonald case. He requested that I attend a briefing at his Palm Beach office on Wednesday afternoon. This was Amanda's case but I was not certain if or how she would participate in the meeting.

When I entered the conference room to meet with

the prosecution team, I was pleased to see Amanda at the table. McDonald continued to insist Jenkins was the mastermind, and the prosecutors wanted to have an air-tight case before any court action.

As the meeting concluded Amanda walked up and said; "Sorry, I have been busy. I originally planned to call into the meeting. The legal team wanted me here in person so I booked an early morning flight."

When we were alone, she asked; "Are you free for dinner? The trip was last minute so I only have this pair of jeans to wear. Dinner will have to be informal."

"Sure, let's meet at the hamburger place on Clematis for a burger and beer. OK?"

"Sounds good, see you at 7:30?"

I arrived early and Amanda greeted me with a friendly hug when she walked up promptly at 7:30. We had just ordered our beers and burgers when Donna's friend walked up, smiled at the two of us, placed a business card on the table and walked away down the sidewalk.

I was completely off-guard and confused by her actions. Amanda was coy; "She certainly enjoyed interrupting. Should I ask how you know her?"

I replied: "I really don't."

I picked up her business card. "Well, I'll be damned. Her name is Lisa Keating and she is an attorney with Alexander's law firm."

"So, what was that about?"

"I don't know. I thought I recognized a friend of hers as the woman with Keith Jones in The Bahamas. In fact, her friend was the woman I was staring at that night we had dinner at Pistache."

"I have been curious about her friend's identity and made a fool of myself trying to meet her on a couple of occasions."

"I was sitting here a week or so ago when she suddenly stopped to ask why I was asking her friend about The Bahamas. It was not a friendly exchange, and she told me her friend was dead."

"All I know is her friend's name was Donna and they are both attorneys."

Amanda asked; "Are you certain this Donna was the same woman with Keith in The Bahamas?"

"There was a photo on the wall at the Yacht Club when I was there on Paradox last spring. I took a photo of the photo with my phone. Let me show you the picture."

Amanda smiled; "Steve, that's not a very good photo for identification. Makes me suspicious you were just trying to pick up an attractive woman in Palm Beach."

"Amanda, at this point, I'm pretty sure it's the same person."

Amanda was skeptical; "Even if it is the same person, this photo doesn't mean they were together. It looks like he is talking to her but she is not looking at him. He could just be trying to pick her up at the bar. Is this the only photo?"

"No, it was the best shot of her so it's the only one I took. You might be right, it wasn't clear they were together in the other photos."

Amanda said; "OK, eat your burger. Enough business talk."

#   #   #

I remained puzzled by the possible connection between Donna and Keith Jones. Did Lisa and Donna both work at Alexander's law firm or were they just friends? Was it possible Jones was having an affair with Donna or was their being at the Yacht Club at the same time just a coincidence?

Why would Lisa give me her business card in such a provocative manner when I was seated with another woman?

I assume, whatever the reason, the next step was up to me. Thursday morning I dialed the direct number listed on Lisa's business card.

A woman answered and said; "Hello."

I responded; "Lisa?"

"Yes."

"This is Steve Wilson, I want to invite you to lunch."

"I don't want to be seen with you" and she hung up her phone.

I sat in silence for a few minutes - this is a very confusing situation. What the hell is going on?

I placed her card on my desk and entered the number in my computer address book. I dropped her card as I picked it up to put it back in my wallet. It landed face down and, for the first time, I noticed another phone number written in pencil on the back of her card.

I didn't think it would be smart to call that number right away - maybe later.

Friday night I fixed dinner on Paradox. After dinner I was sitting on my back deck sipping a cognac and smoking my occasional Cuban cigar. I decided it was time to call that second number - what did I have to lose?

After two rings; "This is Lisa."

"Lisa, this is Steve Wilson."

"About time you looked at the back of my card. I want to ask you some questions."

"OK, I'm listening."

"Why did you ask Donna about The Bahamas?"

"I thought I recognized her from a photo taken at a party at the Staniel Cay Yacht Club. She looked like a woman that had been with a banker that drowned later the same night. I was just curious."

"Why were you curious?"

"You have my card and I assume you have looked at my website. I consult with banks about fraud and that banker was suspected of embezzlement. I was helping the bank with its investigation."

"Lisa, why do you ask?"

"Donna was my friend. I don't believe Donna committed suicide by jumping off her balcony."

Once again she hung up.

Maybe I can learn a little more about Donna - suicide from a balcony would be my next search. I finished my cognac and took my cigar with me for a walk along the waterfront.

On Saturday morning I started my online search for any recent suicide by a woman named Donna. I finally came across a short article in the Palm Beach newspaper:

Residents of an apartment building in West Palm Beach were shocked when they discovered a young woman had either fallen or jumped from her apartment Thursday night. Police identified the woman as Donna Hawkins. The Police confirmed she had an apartment in the building.

My online search located a Donna Hawkins who had graduated with honors from a law school in Indiana and had started her career at a law firm in Cincinnati. The graduation photo certainly resembled the mystery woman, but I wasn't certain. I located no additional information concerning current employment.

Was Donna Hawkins another connection to Alexander?

35

1st Week of November

I took the train to Miami Monday for a meeting with the audit team of a bank that had significant Latin American customer relationships. At our meeting they requested I do an independent evaluation of the bank's money laundering controls.

After signing my standard consulting and confidentiality agreement, the bank provided me with read-only access to their operating systems. This relationship permitted me to test and validate the bank's systems working from my desk on Paradox.

This assignment kept me busy for the balance of the week. My testing on Wednesday revealed several holes in the bank's systems that we were able to plug without finding any illegal activity.

My probing on Thursday was a different story. I identified some very strange customer activity at one of the bank's branch locations. When I brought it to the audit team's attention they were not surprised. They asked that I finish testing and then share my findings at the conclusion of my evaluation.

During our de-briefing on Friday, they revealed they were already aware of the problem and their board had requested they hire me to make certain any other issues were identified. They revealed that the bank was one of the institutions involved in the FBI's major money laundering investigation.

#   #   #

This Miami project consumed most of my daytime hours during the week. In the evenings I took a break from my detailed systems evaluation and spent a little time doing homework on Robert Alexander. The names of Robert and his firm kept popping up and my curiosity had increased with each occasion.

I found it interesting his firm did not have a website but an online search of business directories revealed the firm had offices in Portland, Boston and Palm Beach. I was frustrated that I could not locate a list of attorneys to determine if Donna Hawkins worked for his law firm.

The Portland newspaper had extensive coverage describing a fifty million dollar injury case he had won about ten years ago. The articles all mentioned the name of the hospital in Boston but had no reference to an insurance company.

Alexander had graduated with honors from a university in Boston and the school website listed him as a trustee. I also noticed the university had a building named after Robert Alexander. The only personal property I could locate was his home in Portland and a ninety foot yacht with a home port of Fort Lauderdale.

He was married and had two grown children. His picture appeared regularly at charitable events in Portland, Boston, Palm Beach and Fort Lauderdale. He made generous donations to a number of candidates in both political parties.

He appeared to be a very successful attorney, and I found nothing suspicious in his background. Tory had confirmed the deposits to his firm's account at the Rockland branch were from a major insurance company.

I remained puzzled, why was Keith Jones talking to the woman I suspected was Donna Hawkins at the Staniel Cay Yacht Club? Did Donna also work for Alexander's law firm? If so, was there a connection? Neither Keith nor Donna could tell me - they were both dead.

36

2nd Week of November

Anne called two weeks ago to invite me to visit her for a week in Stone Harbor. I was pleased she called, but Maine was getting cold. I booked my flight to New York with a Saturday night layover so I could pack my warm clothes. My flight to Bangor arrived mid-day Sunday, and I picked up a rental car to drive to Stone Harbor. I made plans to return to New York from Portland on Saturday.

When I arrived, Anne seemed happy to see me. She greeted me with a big hug and kiss. She appeared very relaxed and said business at the Inn was winding down and we could relax for a few days.

Anne was two different people on occasions - she could be a romantic lover one day and a cold business woman the next. She was always charming to her guests, but she was preoccupied on our boat trip in June and distant with me after we returned to the Inn. Anne's greeting was a welcome change.

We had dinner at Fisherman's Restaurant Sunday night and visited with friends that stopped by our table to say hello. We returned to the Inn and snuggled with glasses of cognac in front her wood-burning fireplace before going to bed.

The next morning Anne said, "I want to visit Acadia Park again. It's a beautiful place and our plans last year didn't work out as anticipated. I have booked a room at an Inn in Bar Harbor for two nights so we can make our visit a relaxing journey."

Rocky Shoreline of Acadia National Park

As I drove toward Bar Harbor, she told me she wanted to be back on Thursday to talk to some folks about winter preparations for the Inn.

Our drive around Acadia was uneventful this year

and we laughed as we enjoyed our walks along the rugged shoreline without interruption. Anne arranged dinner Tuesday evening at a waterfront restaurant that received five-star reviews. I was pleasantly surprised she didn't make our stay in Bar Harbor a competitive research project. She was relaxed - we enjoyed a romantic evening.

Anne turned more serious on our drive back to Stone Harbor late Wednesday.

"Steve, I can't tell you how much I enjoyed the last couple of days. I was ready for a break."

"It's been a year and I think it's time we talk about our relationship. I enjoy being with you and, at the present time, there is no other man in my life. This is difficult to say, but I don't see how we can bridge our differences and make our relationship any more permanent."

I was not anticipating a relationship conversation and was rather nervous and uncomfortable. I asked; "What do you mean?"

"Steve, I love Maine and only plan a couple of brief visits to Florida. I would get bored if I didn't have my boat and the Inn to manage. I adore my new friends in Maine. I hated the idea of coming here when my husband retired but it has been the best thing for me. I don't want that to change."

"On the other hand, you love being on your new boat in Florida. It's clear from our few conversations that you find your new business exciting. Your life has changed dramatically since we first met. You would be very unhappy being a year-round retired Maine resident. We just don't fit together long term."

I started to reply; "Anne".

"Please, let me finish. I want you to know I am happy with our relationship just the way it is - I am not suggesting a change. You have been single for over twenty years and manage to get along just fine. I don't want to mislead you or drive you away. I like spending time on vacation together."

"Finally, Ken and Frances have invited me to join them for Thanksgiving and I hope you will join us."

She concluded; "That's my story - what do you think?"

"Anne, I don't know what to say. I think you are probably right but is it OK if I take time to think about it?"

"You don't need to respond, it won't change how I feel. Now let's have another nice evening together before you go back to Florida."

#   #   #

Anne was all business again Thursday morning, so I booked a hotel in Portland and made plans to have lunch with James Parker on Friday. Our past conversations had only focused on business and I wanted to know James a little better.

I thought about calling Amanda but decided it was not a good idea on such short notice as I had not told her I was coming to Maine. Portland has a nationally recognized restaurant scene, so it was easy for me to select a waterfront location to enjoy a seafood dinner Thursday night.

I met James at his office late Friday morning and he arranged a brief meeting with Tory.

Tory reported; "Steve, I am not finished my calculations, but your suspicions about Keith's gambling losses appears to be correct. The credit card banks were reluctant to cooperate until I assured them we had a full recovery of the embezzled funds and I was not trying to recover any money from them. I have just received copies of his credit card statements and they show significant transactions at two casinos in Maine and at Atlantis Resort over in Nassau."

James and I then walked a short distance to a private business club for lunch. We shared stories about college, early career, family, charities and current banking events. The more we talked, the more I liked him as he had a wide variety of interests and loved his hometown of Portland.

We were still at our table enjoying a cup of coffee when James said; "Hello Robert, good to see you. You still enjoy that boat of yours?"

"Sure do, every chance I get."

"Steve, let me introduce you to Robert Alexander. Robert, I want to introduce you to Steve Wilson, he is a consultant from New York we retain at the bank."

"Good to meet you Mr. Wilson."

I replied; "Actually, we met briefly a while back at Palm Harbor Marina. I was sitting with Ken Stewart on his boat one afternoon."

Alexander paused; "Sorry, I don't recall. Do you have a boat?"

"Yes, I have a custom Maine lobster boat currently docked at Palm Harbor."

"Interesting, we take our boat up to Palm Beach occasionally when I have client meetings. I hate to stay in hotels. What kind of consulting do you do?"

James answered; "Steve is a fraud specialist. He uncovered that embezzlement last year down at Rockland. You might remember the young banker that drowned in The Bahamas."

Alexander sat down at our table and answered; "Faintly, I think he was a college friend of my son. I think we moved a couple of accounts down to his branch as a favor."

James answered; "That's right. You might recall the bank had to confirm your balances after we discovered the embezzlement. Fortunately, your accounts were not involved."

Alexander responded; "Yes, thankfully they were not involved. I heard you recovered all the money, is that correct?"

James added; "Yes, that's right. In fact, we recovered a little more money than he embezzled. Mystery why he did it if he didn't need the money."

Alexander turned to me; "Any theories?"

I responded; "Not really, we located some unusual transactions at a bank in Boston but have not yet traced the source."

Alexander commented; "Really an unfortunate story. My son said he was a good kid."

I decided to take a chance; "Robert, I'm curious, did an attorney named Donna Hawkins work for your firm in Palm Beach?"

Alexander looked startled; "Yes, tragic situation. She recently committed suicide."

With that Alexander stood; "Good to meet you Mr. Wilson, here's my card. Do you have one? Maybe we will meet again on the docks."

We exchanged cards, and he walked to the exit.

As we walked out of the club; "Steve, I am glad you had an opportunity to meet Robert. Sounds like you might have other friends in common."

"By the way, my wife and I have no plans for dinner. We could also invite Amanda."

"Thank you, but I already booked my reservation to fly back to New York."

This was the first time I had an opportunity to visit with and observe Alexander. He was shorter than I thought and pudgy. His pinstriped suit and vest were too small for his weight. He appeared friendly but struck me as vain and self-important.

Alexander had just confirmed that Donna had worked for his law firm. Why was she with Keith in The Bahamas?

37

3rd Week of November

I unpacked my Maine travel gear and took the opportunity to visit with a few friends over the weekend in New York. On Monday I was on a flight back to Palm Beach without a suitcase - everything I needed was already on Paradox.

I had a busy week of conference calls as I worked to complete paperwork related to my various consulting assignments before the holidays.

I didn't spot Lisa on any of my walks, at a bar or while having dinner on Clematis.

I was surprised when Alexander stopped at my slip Wednesday evening and said; "Hello, so this is your lobster boat."

"That's right, welcome aboard."

"No thanks, I just arrived and I have dinner plans and I've got a meeting tomorrow morning before I return to Portland. I want to spend Thanksgiving next week with my family."

I watched as he walked down the dock to his yacht tied up on the T-head, the extra long section at the far end of the dock for large yachts. Alexander was wearing a business suit and looked out of place on the marina docks.

Alexander always appeared relaxed and friendly when I had been introduced to him but I thought his actions felt superficial. I was surprised he remembered me and my boat. Ken was right, people do tend to be nicer on the docks. I was relieved Ken's investment account with Alexander was legitimate.

The balance of my week was busy with calls and paperwork. I enjoyed my growing consulting practice, but it was beginning to feel like work. I was looking forward to the holiday season.

Anne made arrangements to fly to Palm Beach to meet me before we joined Ken and Frances for Thanksgiving. She arrived Saturday afternoon and our plan was to take Paradox to Fort Lauderdale if the weather was favorable. Otherwise, we would take the train as I had found no reason to rent a car.

I wanted to do something special when Anne arrived, so I made a reservation to take her to

Pistache for dinner on Sunday night. We both avoided any relationship conversation at dinner and I was relieved she appeared to be in a romantic mood.

We both gasped when we stepped aboard Paradox and found a dead cat on the back deck. The cat had a yellow ribbon tied around its neck with a gift card attached. I felt nauseous as I retrieved a plastic trash bag for the dead cat and removed the gift card. A short, hand printed note was inside.

"Curiosity killed the cat."

I did not share the contents of the gift card with Anne and she didn't ask to see it.

Anne was traumatized and sat down inside the boat while I disposed of the cat inside the trash bag. When I returned, I sat next to Anne and tried to comfort her but I found my hands were shaking.

4th Week of November - Thanksgiving

The weather was not favorable for a comfortable offshore passage so we took the train to Fort Lauderdale on Tuesday morning. We were both disturbed by finding the dead cat and ready for a change of venue. I said nothing about the dead cat to Ken or Frances when we arrived in Fort Lauderdale.

Frances also invited other friends to join us for Thanksgiving dinner and she had set a festive table for ten people to share a traditional turkey feast on Thursday. Frances enjoys cooking and we all enjoyed her wonderful meal with sweet potatoes, broccoli, creamed corn, asparagus, cranberry sauce and pumpkin pie for dessert.

Thanksgiving Day was a great diversion, and I put the cat out of my mind for the day. Anne was troubled the entire visit, and any thought of romance had disappeared.

Anne planned to return to Maine on Saturday morning and I noticed she and Frances had a long talk on Friday afternoon. The four of us shared dinner at a noisy waterfront restaurant Friday night. The music was entertaining but too loud for conversation.

Saturday morning we thanked Ken and Frances for a wonderful Thanksgiving holiday. Ken drove Anne to the Fort Lauderdale airport for her flight back to Maine and then dropped me off at the train station for my return to Palm Beach.

Ken's parting comment was; "We really enjoy your company, thanks for coming. Sorry about the cat."

38

1st Week of December

To say the least, I was troubled by the message that accompanied the dead cat. None of my current assignments appeared to be related; Jenkins was dead, McDonald was in custody, and Amanda had the other cases in Maine and Florida under control.

Alexander's client accounts were legitimate arrangements with insurance companies - or were they? As I recalled, Tory had only confirmed that an insurance company was the source of funds for the payments to Ken. What about the transactions in the other account?

On Monday morning I called Tory;

"Tory, when you checked those accounts for Alexander in Rockland - did you check just the one or both of them?"

"Just the one with a payment to Kenneth Stewart

that you asked about - why?"

"Not sure, could you check the source of funds for the second account?"

"Sure, I will call you back shortly."

When Tory called she reported; "Steve, monthly distributions were made to eight individuals from the second account. However, the funds for that second account did not come from an insurance company. They were wires from an account with a bank in Boston."

"Do you know the name on the account?"

"The wire transfer said the funds came from an account called Settlement Investments."

"Tory, thanks for the help. That's all I need for now."

I felt stupid. Why hadn't I been thorough and asked Tory to look at both accounts the first time? Now I needed to identify the ownership and source of funds related to Settlement Investments. No evidence suggested the source of funds wasn't related to an insurance company so the transactions could still be legitimate.

Alexander was no doubt an important customer at the bank in Boston and I didn't want to create any undo suspicion. I was stumped and uncertain how best to proceed.

It was time to ask for some advice and I called Mark. He was busy all day and said he would call me about eight o'clock when he had time to talk.

"Steve, you can always get my attention when you say you might have uncovered a major Ponzi scheme. What have you found?"

It took me almost an hour to go step-by-step with my suspicions starting with the death of Jones, the photo on the Yacht Club wall, the suspicious suicide of Donna, the strange conversations with Lisa, the wire transfers from The Bahamas into the account Jones had established at the bank in Boston, the legitimate source of funds for Ken's investment, the questionable source of funds for the second account, my conversation with Alexander and finally, the dead cat with the gift note.

Mark was silent for a moment and then said; "Steve that's a complex web of circumstantial evidence. Let me think about this overnight and I will call you tomorrow."

I generally sleep well but I was restless the entire night. I was extremely troubled by the dead cat on my boat. It reminded me of a horror movie. For the first time I didn't feel safe on Paradox. My hands trembled as I made certain the cabin door was locked each night.

Mark called mid-morning Tuesday; "Steve, you don't have enough for us to get a court order to look at any of those accounts. Any chance you can uncover more information without alerting Alexander?"

"Not certain, I don't know the senior auditor at the bank in Boston very well and we don't seem to get along for some reason. I think any contact will alert Alexander."

"That's what I thought but I think that's our only alternative today. If everything is legit, you will have a lot of explaining to do and will need to make apologies to Alexander. If the transactions are not legit, then we can open an investigation."

"Now, I am seriously concerned about the message with that dead cat on your boat. It looks like you kicked a hornets' nest even if it's not related to Alexander. As you know, I don't have any agents free in Florida so I have already notified Amanda she is to go down to Palm Beach. Stay safe."

"OK, I will think of a way to contact the bank in Boston this afternoon and keep you in the loop."

"Keep Amanda in the loop. Stay safe."

Amanda called me about fifteen minutes later and

asked; "Steve, what kind of mess has your curiosity got you into this time? Mark called and told me to book a flight to Palm Beach. He said you might be in serious trouble. My flight arrives at six tonight. What the hell is going on?"

"It's a long and complex story that starts with the death of Keith Jones. We can talk tonight. I need to prepare an audit request for Tory to send to the bank in Boston."

I expected all hell to break loose when Alexander found out about the request. I was certain he had a good relationship with the bank in Boston and they would inform him. The bank didn't even have to honor the audit request to achieve my objective of antagonizing Alexander.

Most criminals panic when they think their scam is discovered. If my suspicions were right, I expected Alexander to make a stupid move and give the FBI a reason to act.

I drafted an audit confirmation request, but to be effective it had to be a request from the bank in Portland related to the Jones embezzlement. I emailed my proposed request to James and followed up with a call. I asked him to have Tory join our discussion. Tory's office was nearby and she entered his office a few minutes later.

I explained; "James, the transactions in the second

232

account are very typical of a Ponzi scheme. I am concerned there could be a link between Keith Jones and Alexander."

"When I visited The Bahamas last Spring I saw a photo of Keith with a woman who I believe was Donna Hawkins, a female attorney that worked for Alexander's firm. It's troubling to me that Jones and Hawkins have both died under mysterious circumstances."

"To protect the bank, Tory needs to request account information from the bank in Boston. We need to determine if those money transfers are legitimate transactions. If not, was Keith involved with the scam? Why was he with Donna in The Bahamas?"

James was concerned; "What happens if everything is legit when Alexander finds out about this request? He will be livid and move his accounts."

"You can blame me and I will take responsibility."

James concluded; "We don't really have a choice if I want to protect the bank - do we?"

"No, we don't have a choice. If this is a fraud, then you need to know if Keith was involved."

39

James and Tory called me back late that afternoon and Tory reported;

"Steve, I sent the request to the attention of my former classmate that did all the previous research related to the Jones embezzlement. I received a routine response by confidential email with the information we requested. She didn't even call me. She handled my follow-up audit in the normal course of business."

"I posted her response on our confidential internal information system so you can read it but I can summarize. All the deposits into that account are wired from an account at a bank in The Bahamas. That account in Nassau has the same name, Settlement Investments. It may be circumstantial, but that's the same bank that wired funds to the account Keith set up at the bank in Boston."

Just then I could overhear Parker's assistant interrupt; "Mr. Parker, the President of a bank in Boston is on the phone and he sounds really upset.

He insists he talk to you right away."

"Steve, did you hear that? I think we've kicked the hornets' nest. Go ahead, put him on line two."

I was put on hold for several minutes then James returned to my call;

"The officer assigned to Alexander's accounts was notified by the bank's audit department about our request. The account officer apparently went ballistic when he was told the response had already been sent back to our bank. From what the President said to me, it sounded like the account officer called Alexander and Alexander called the President raising hell. The President had the account officer with him when he called me."

"I told them I understood it was a routine audit request related to the Jones embezzlement and I would look into it. They did most of the talking."

"I expect a visit from Alexander any minute. I will let you know what happens. Tory, you should go back to your office and stay out of sight."

James called me back in about thirty minutes.

"Alexander showed up at my office about ten minutes after we hung up. He was angry as hell. Never seen him use that kind of language and he made all kinds of legal threats against the bank. As we agreed, I told him it was a routine audit request you had initiated as part of the Keith Jones embezzlement investigation. The last thing he said was 'that son of a bitch' when he left my office."

I replied; "Thanks for the update. I assume you understand his reaction and the fact those wire transfers came from an offshore bank in The Bahamas rather than an insurance company most likely confirms my suspicions?"

"Sadly, I do."

Amanda's flight was due in about an hour. I left a message on her cell phone to call me when she landed. The dead cat had me spooked, and I didn't want to stay on Paradox overnight so I packed an overnight bag. I felt safer in a public location and walked up to Pistache. I sat at the bar to await Amanda's call.

When Amanda called, I told her to meet me at the restaurant and I would bring her up-to-date over dinner. As I watched the door for Amanda, I saw Lisa walk in and look around. When she spotted me she started to leave but hesitated at the door.

Lisa turned and approached me. She looked distraught; "I just got off the phone with Robert Alexander. What the hell did you do? He is really pissed at you."

"I sent a routine audit request to the firm's bank in Boston." Lisa was quiet and looked concerned.

Just then Amanda arrived and surveyed the scene; "Hello Steve, who's your friend?"

I was still watching Lisa's reaction and didn't know what to say.

Lisa gathered her composure and said; "I need to go" and walked out the door.

"Steve, what's going on?"

"We have a private corner table reserved. Let's go to the table to talk." Amanda gave me an inquisitive look when I picked up my overnight bag.

After we were seated at our table, I looked at Amanda and asked; "What did Mark tell you?"

"Not much. He said all his agents in Florida are busy and it's essential I get on a plane and go to Palm Beach. Call Steve for more information. That's it."

"OK. I will start at the beginning with Keith Jones."

I talked most of dinner and described events up to and including her encounter with Lisa at the bar.

"That's it, everything is still circumstantial, but we certainly got a reaction. I think the information in the audit request will be sufficient to get some type of court order but Alexander will likely resist. I don't know how skilled his firm might be and they could create significant delays."

"In any event, I am exhausted and don't feel safe on my boat. I honestly don't know if it's related to Alexander but that business with the dead cat unnerved me."

Amanda said; "Relax, I will make a few calls and arrange a hotel. I think you know, I always carry my FBI ID and a gun in my backpack."

She smiled; "Relax, Mark told me this could be a witness protection assignment. It's my job to keep you safe."

I was relieved. Amanda quickly arranged two adjoining rooms under her name at a nearby hotel. "If anyone checks, you are not registered."

She carefully examined both rooms when we arrived at the hotel. As she stood in the doorway that adjoins the rooms she smiled and said; "It's been a long day and I need my beauty sleep. Don't you dare come through this door unless your life is in danger."

#   #   #

I had difficulty going to sleep and was startled when my phone rang in the middle of the night. I was very apprehensive. I didn't recognize the number but answered; "Hello". The phone was silent, so I hung up.

I had only been awake for a few minutes Wednesday morning when Amanda knocked on the door between our rooms.

"Steve, you up and awake?"

"Yes, and hungry. Give me a minute to get dressed."

When I opened the door she asked; "How did you sleep? You looked exhausted last night."

"Not well, and my phone rang in the middle of the night."

"Who called?"

"No one said a word. Guess it was a wrong number."

Amanda said; "Let's check, look at recent calls on your phone."

"Do you recognize the number?"

"No, but it's local, let me think."

The caller's name would have appeared on my cell phone screen if the number was in my address book. I looked at a few cards and notes I had in my wallet to see if I could find a match.

"Amanda, that's the number for Lisa's cell phone. I only entered her law office numbers in my address book. Stupid, I didn't think to add her cell phone number after I saw it on the back of her card."

"Why do you think she called you in the middle of the night?"

"No, idea."

"Let's order coffee and breakfast from room service and I need to make a few calls. We got a big break late yesterday."

"The President of the bank in Boston called the Boston FBI office about eight o'clock last night. We have an internal system that works off keywords we use when an investigation is opened. It works like an automated internet search."

"I opened a case file for Alexander's law firm last night. Early this morning I got a link to the agent's notes about last night's call."

"The President of the bank said he was concerned about the actions of one of his officers. He told the agent he had just concluded a meeting with the officer and the head of his internal audit department and discovered some very disturbing transactions. The senior auditor will file a formal report today but the President wanted to alert the agent directly to stress the potential importance."

"To summarize, the bank's officer has been seriously compromised by Alexander. The agent's notes indicate the bank officer admitted Alexander was secretly paying for his kids to go to college among other favors. As a result, the officer was finding it easy to overlook some unusual transactions."

"Your audit request surfaced some of those transactions and the bank officer panicked and called Alexander."

"The President told the agent he was confused by the angry reaction of both the bank's officer and Alexander. After his call with Parker he asked his senior auditor to bring a copy of the audit request and response to his office so they could all review the documents together."

"He said he knew something was wrong once he questioned the account officer about the wire transfers from the bank in The Bahamas. He said the account officer confessed to receiving payments from Alexander after he told the senior auditor to do more analysis."

"We should learn more today and this will give us the ammunition we need to go to court later today and at least request an order for Alexander to produce his records. It's probably not enough for an arrest warrant."

I added; "I am concerned we know so little and Alexander has been alerted. We have no idea how much money might be involved and where it might be located."

Amanda responded; "After we eat, why don't you return that call from Lisa?"

40

I guess fear makes me hungry. I was starved and ate a full breakfast when it arrived. Amanda seemed happy with an English muffin and yogurt.

After eating, I touched the return call button on my cell phone and a sleepy voice answered; "Hello."

"This is Steve Wilson, did you call me last night?"

After a long silence; "Yes, I think we need to talk."

"When and where?"

"Soon in a safe place."

"How about the local FBI office?"

"Not a chance, how about Starbucks on Clematis? I think a busy public location will be safe."

"OK, what time? Is it OK if my lady friend comes with me? She can sit at another table if that's OK with you."

"Sure, see you in an hour" and she discontinued the call.

#   #   #

Amanda and I arrived early to find a high-top table where we could sit more discreetly inside. After a few minutes we grabbed a table when two people stood up to leave.

Lisa arrived a little early also and carefully looked over the crowd from the entrance. She waited until Amanda moved to one of the empty chairs near the front.

Lisa then got in line and ordered a coffee. She looked over the crowd one more time before she joined me at my table.

Lisa was quiet for a time and I waited for her to speak. Finally she said; "Can we talk? I don't know what's happening and I am getting scared."

"Sure, maybe I can help."

"Like I told you at Pistache, Alexander called yesterday evening. He was out of control. He has always been calm and professional - the call was really out of character."

"He called you a nosy son of a bitch and wanted to know if you ever talked to Donna. When I told him 'yes' he went ballistic and hung up."

"A few minutes later the firm's accountant called me and said to make certain Donna's office was completely empty. I said it was and reminded him Alexander's boat captain had packed up her laptop and all her files and sent them to Portland. He just said; 'good' and hung up."

"I called one of the other estate attorneys I know in Portland. I asked her what the hell was going on? She said she didn't know but had overheard Alexander shouting at a banker about an audit request from some bastard in Florida. She said he told his assistant to shred the files in his safe and he left the office and didn't return."

"That's when I decided I needed a drink, walked over to Pistache and saw you at the bar."

I asked; "Why are you scared?"

"Alexander's boat captain left a message on my cell phone while I was talking to my friend in Portland. His message said; 'Don't be stupid, if you know what's good for you, don't talk'."

"Mr. Wilson, I have no contact with that man but I know Donna didn't like him. I always thought he was trying to get her in bed."

I asked; "Lisa, what do you do at the law firm?"

"Just what it says on my business card. I plan

estates for clients."

"What did Donna do?"

"She worked with Alexander on his settlement accounts. She always said the insurance companies require strict confidentiality, so we didn't talk about her clients."

"I know she helped Alexander arrange investors when the damage victims wanted cash upfront and the insurance companies wanted to pay over time. She always wanted to know if my clients had extra cash to invest."

I asked; "What do you want me to do?"

"I want you to tell me what's happening. Is the firm in trouble? Am I in trouble? Why did his captain threaten me?"

"Lisa, I can't say much except I discovered a discrepancy in one of those investment accounts."

"That's what I suspected. I need an attorney."

"Lisa, my lady friend is an FBI agent. Do you want to talk to her?"

"Only after I have an attorney but I'm smart enough to know it's best if I cooperate. I don't believe I have done anything wrong."

"Lisa, what do you want to do next?"

"I don't know. I'm afraid to go home and I stayed with a friend last night. I don't want to end up like Donna."

This was a change in topic; "What do you think happened with Donna?"

"I don't know, but I just can't believe she committed suicide."

"If that's the case let's talk to my friend - she can help and you don't need to say any more until you retain an attorney."

After a long pause she said; "OK".

I signaled Amanda to join us and said; "Lisa wants to cooperate, but she has not yet retained an attorney. I have told her you are an agent and it's best if she makes no official statement to you. She doesn't feel safe and wants protection. What can you do?"

Amanda turned to Lisa, offered a friendly smile and said; "Hi, my name is Amanda Smith and I am a Special Agent with the FBI. Steve is right, please do not say anything about this case to me until you have retained an attorney. You will be safe in our local office and we can put you in a private room so you can locate and talk privately to an attorney.

Is that OK with you?"

Lisa relaxed; "Yes, but I don't want to be seen on the street with him."

Amanda replied; "No problem, I will walk you to our office. Steve, please stay here until I get back. I don't want you out walking alone."

Amanda returned in about an hour and said; "Thanks, I don't want to ask about what she told you and potentially compromise her testimony if we need it. Let's go back to the hotel."

# # #

Back at the hotel I watched as Amanda sat with her laptop and made phone calls. Mark had designated her agent in charge and she was getting frequent reports from the field.

An agent from Boston had been assigned to investigate Alexander's accounts and was now working at the bank with the bank's audit team.

Alexander had departed Portland at midnight on his private jet headed to Fort Lauderdale but the jet diverted in flight to Nassau. The aircraft landed in the early morning and Alexander was no longer at the airport.

A judge in Boston had not yet authorized the FBI to

seize Alexander's records but agents were being authorized to declare the firm's offices and Alexander's boat as possible crime scenes.

Police officers in Fort Lauderdale reported the yacht did not appear to be occupied when they arrived to place the Do Not Cross tape along the dock. They did not enter and search the yacht.

Amanda got a call from the local FBI office that Lisa had retained an attorney and after spending time with her attorney they provided a written statement. Lisa's attorney then departed with Lisa.

Amanda let me read Lisa's statement in a secure folder on her laptop. When I finished reading I told her the statement was consistent with our conversation at Starbucks.

It had been a long, busy day and Amanda ordered dinner for the two of us and a beer for me from room service.

About ten o'clock Amanda walked to the door between our rooms and she smiled before closing the door;

"Remember, knock only if your life is in danger."

41

Thursday morning dawned bright and clear. I was going stir crazy with my adrenaline on high and not much to do while Amanda coordinated the investigation.

I was relieved when after finishing another room service breakfast she said; "OK, it's time to put you to work. You are now working as a consultant to the FBI."

Just then a young man from room service knocked to pick up our tray and ask what else we needed before the maid came to clean the room. We couldn't help notice his sly smile when he said; "You guys ever going outside?" and winked.

Amanda just gave him her own sly smile and replied; "Not today, we are having way too much fun" and she winked back at the kid.

Amanda just laughed when he blushed and closed the door; "Cheeky kid."

Amanda logged me on her network; "Go to work."

I was ready to do something useful and started reviewing the Boston agent's report and the account information from the bank in Boston.

The file Amanda opened also included the statement from the bank officer that had managed Alexander's accounts. His was a sad story of steady compromise. It started with simple favors like tickets to a sports event and ended with secret accounts to pay for his kid's education and family vacations. The favors served Alexander's purpose and the account officer stopped asking questions. It was also clear the law firm's accountant had arranged all the payments.

The bank account information was a complex web of interconnected accounts and transactions. If it had been legitimate, I would have complemented the law firm's accountant for his imagination.

After several hours of analysis, I announced; "Amanda, I am ready to review my financial summary with you."

She replied; "Thanks, let's do it."

"Alexander's accountant established a separate bank account for each settlement transaction. As a result, it was easy for me to separate the legitimate investment accounts funded by an insurance company from the fake accounts."

"Six of the early investment accounts, such as the account with Ken Stewart, are legitimate. The law firm's clients received one hundred million dollars from the investment groups organized by Alexander. In return, the firm's clients assigned two hundred million dollars of future insurance payments to the investment groups."

"These investment groups are structured to provide each investor an annual return of about ten percent over the term of their investment. For example, Ken invested three million dollars and, over a period of years, he will receive six million dollars in payments from the insurance company."

"Alexander's law firm is entitled to thirty percent of the settlements as their fee. This amount is also being paid to the law firm over a period of years. His firm has been receiving about five million dollars each year from the insurance settlements."

"The problem developed when Alexander added offices and started spending more than five million dollars per year to pay for his yacht and jet. I suspect he spent this money expecting to settle more large damage claims - settlements that did not occur. He simply started running out of cash."

"To replenish his cash, he started with a fake settlement for fifty million dollars. As you know, once someone starts a Ponzi scheme, it's almost impossible to stop. Over time, he needed even more money to cover his expenses and repay his investors."

Alexander Law > Settlement Accounts Summary ($000)				
6 > Legitimate Investor Accounts				
Insurance Settlements	Investor Accounts	Paid To Investors	Remaining Amount Due	Investor Total Payout
$200,000	$100,000	$100,000	$100,000	$200,000
12 > Ponzi Scheme Accounts				
$0	$800,000	$400,000	$1,200,000	$1,600,000
Alexander Cash Flow > Ponzi Scheme Accounts				
Cash Investment from Investors	$800,000			
Less: Payments to Investors	($400,000)			
Net Cash Flow from Investors	$400,000			
Less: Cash Transfers from Ponzi Scheme Accounts				
Pay: Office & Personal Expenses	($5,000)			
Pay: Yacht Purchase & Expenses	($10,000)			
Pay: Jet Lease & Expenses	($10,000)			
Political Donations: Local & National	($5,000)			
University Donations	($10,000)			
Transfers to Bank in Bahamas?	($350,000)			
Remaining Balance: Bank in Boston	$10,000			

"Alexander created a total of twelve fake settlements that now total eight hundred million dollars. He has paid these investors four hundred million dollars to date; but he doesn't have the funds to repay the remaining $1.2 billion he still owes these investors!"

"I have traced forty million dollars he has withdrawn from these Ponzi scheme accounts to help pay his extra expenses for the yacht, the private jet, political contributions, office expansion, large donations and his personal expenses. He also diverted three hundred fifty million dollars to the bank in The Bahamas. The account in Boston has a remaining balance of ten million dollars."

"I can fill in the gaps and document more of the expenses once we get the accounting records from the law firm. At this time, I have no idea what happened to the money he transferred to The Bahamas."

Amanda said; "Steve, well done. This analysis provides all the information we need to obtain a court order."

It was now noon and room service delivered sandwiches for lunch. As we were eating;

"Steve, I arranged an interview with Lisa at three o'clock this afternoon at our offices. I want you to observe the interview."

Shortly after three o'clock I was sitting outside Amanda's small interview room with one of the prosecuting attorneys. We could both listen and observe Amanda's interview through a one-way mirror.

Lisa and her attorney were sitting at a small table across from Amanda. The room was empty except for the table and three chairs. I noticed that Amanda was not taking notes and had no papers on the table.

Amanda started her interview in a very relaxed and friendly manner noting Lisa had volunteered to the interview. However, Amanda did read Lisa her rights to insure everything related to the interview was conducted properly.

Amanda began her questions; "Lisa as you know, you are not the subject of this investigation. However, we believe you might have information that will be helpful and we understand you have agreed to cooperate. As your attorney has probably advised you, withholding information is not advisable."

"Let me start by asking if you were acquainted with Keith Jones?"

"No, I never met him."

"But you know who he was, correct?"

"Yes, he was a banker from Maine."

"Did your friend Donna Hawkins know Keith?"

"Yes, she did."

"It might save time if you describe their relationship. Can you do that?"

Lisa looked at her attorney, then answered; "Yes, I will tell you what I know. I think Donna only met him once or maybe twice over in The Bahamas. I know she didn't want to go on that last trip but Alexander insisted."

"Do you know how she got to Staniel Cay on that last trip? They have no record of her arrival or departure."

"Yes, we talked before she went. She told me she was going to fly with Alexander to Nassau on his jet and then they would take his yacht to some island. Alexander wanted her to meet that banker and persuade him to stop making trouble."

Amanda asked; "How?"

Lisa was irritated; "I don't know but she wasn't going to sleep with him. Donna was a flirt but not a prostitute."

"Do you know what happened?"

"No, I asked her about the trip but Donna didn't

want to talk when she got back. She did say they just anchored out and didn't go to the island."

"Donna was really upset. The whole experience left her on edge. She said Keith was stubborn and arrogant. He didn't want to cooperate with her. But that was all, she didn't want to say any more about the trip."

"When did you find out Keith was dead?"

"I liked Donna, she was my friend. We didn't work together but we would go out for drinks and talk. She liked to flirt. I was her safety net. You know, a pretty woman like you or Donna goes out with a rather plain friend like me."

Amanda asked again; "When did you find out Keith was dead?"

After a pause; "The night your friend asked Donna about The Bahamas. After she walked out of the bar she broke down and cried. Donna said she didn't think anybody would remember she had been with Keith the night he was killed."

"The official report said Keith's death was an accidental drowning - why did Donna say killed?"

"She wouldn't say any more and told me to forget what she said. She was still crying when we walked to her apartment building."

"How did she get back to Florida?"

"Donna told me they took the yacht back to Nassau and she and Alexander returned to Palm Beach on his jet."

"Do you know who was on the yacht?"

"I think only Alexander, Donna and the captain - she didn't mention anyone else."

"What do you think happened to Donna?"

"Like I said, I don't believe she committed suicide like Alexander has suggested. She was upset about what happened in The Bahamas but Donna didn't kill herself."

"Did you say Donna was afraid of the captain?"

"Yes, she never liked him, but after the trip to The Bahamas she was really frightened by him."

"Do you know where the captain might be today?"

"No, if I had to guess he is also long gone. My friends at the office in Portland said Alexander took his jet to Nassau and disappeared."

"Lisa, you have been helpful, thank you. Is there anything else you want to tell me today?"

Lisa looked at her attorney, he nodded and she replied; "I wasn't too surprised when I heard your friend's audit request made Alexander really angry. I was starting to suspect Donna was organizing more settlement funds than the number of damage cases the firm had actually settled."

Amanda stood up; "Thank you Lisa, we will likely have more questions but that's enough for today."

#   #   #

Amanda and I walked back to the hotel. She listened to the recording of her interview and added some notes on her laptop before we discussed Lisa's answers.

Once she finished; "Steve, what do you think?"

"It certainly sounds like Keith uncovered their scam and was being paid-off by Alexander. That would account for the wire transfers to Keith's account from the bank in The Bahamas. It looks like Keith could have been using that money wired from The Bahamas to pay back the funds he embezzled. Tory's work indicates he used the embezzled funds to cover gambling losses."

"It also sounds like something went wrong that night in The Bahamas. Alexander wouldn't have invited Donna if the plan was to kill Jones."

Amanda said she thought it would be our last night at the hotel. Shortly after we finished a late room service dinner she smiled and said;

"Don't knock unless your life is in danger."

42

Friday morning was too nice a day to remain in a hotel room. But, we had work to finish.

My morning was consumed with documenting the flow of funds to provide a more detailed description for the federal prosecutors.

Shortly before noon, Amanda updated me on the case; "The law firm's accountant has been arrested. Both the firm's accountant and Alexander's account officer at the bank in Boston have agreed to cooperate. Criminal charges will depend on the value of their testimony."

"Lisa's statement was helpful but provided no incriminating evidence. I suspect there is more to her story."

"The judge authorized the FBI to seize files in the law firm's offices, Alexander's home and on his yacht. Our agents discovered what appeared to be an incomplete job of shredding documents in each location. There was also an open empty safe on

Alexander's yacht."

"Alexander is presumed to have departed Nassau on a fake passport and the whereabouts of the captain remains a mystery. Alexander has been our focus but Lisa's interview moved the search for the captain to a higher priority."

After eating another bland room service lunch, she called Mark to see if he had any follow-up questions. Amanda's flurry of activity was winding down and she updated her status report.

Late Friday afternoon Amanda said; "The case is coming together, and it's safe to get you out of this room. We both have a bad case of cabin fever. Let's take a walk. I can stay in touch on my cell phone."

It was a cool evening, and we were ready to stay outside. We were both wearing jeans, so we stopped to get a beer and dinner on the outside deck at Bradley's. It had been a busy and tense few days, and we were both ready to wind-down and relax.

Slowly but surely the conversation shifted from the case and became more personal.

"Steve, thanks for respecting my privacy. I appreciate you not knocking on my door at the hotel. Frankly, I'm not certain how I might have responded. I had a very difficult breakup several years ago with a co-worker and have avoided any thoughts of a relationship with a colleague again. He was a nice guy, but I hated having to face him every day at work."

"Steve, did you ever date anybody at the bank?"

"Yes, for a short while, but with my audit job any relationship could end up as a conflict of interest. It just didn't work, but we didn't see each other very frequently in the office. I understand what you mean."

"Have you ever dated a younger woman? Someone my age?"

"Not recently, but yes I dated younger women over the years. However, I never developed a meaningful relationship after my divorce. I think you know we divorced when I moved to Chicago with my job and she wanted to remain in Louisville with friends and family."

"Basically, I was always working and too busy to take a relationship seriously. However, I was acquainted with enough people that I could generally arrange a date for the theater or other social event."

"How busy do you want to be with your new consulting work?"

"I like the flexibility consulting provides. I can generally select assignments and work with people I like. But, honestly, this first year has been busier than I expected."

"Have you decided where you want to live?"

"New York is still home but I realize I'm not spending much time in the city. That might change with time but not yet. I enjoy being on Paradox but she won't be a full-time home for me."

"Do you realize you haven't invited me to see Paradox?"

"Yes, I wasn't certain how you would interpret such an invitation. I didn't want to compromise our working relationship."

"Steve, let's finish here and take a walk to Paradox. I would love to see your boat."

Amanda took my hand as we walked along the waterfront toward the docks. I used my pass card to open the security gate, and we stopped to look across the docks and admire the yachts in the marina. Paradox was probably the smallest boat at the docks.

Amanda turned and gave me a soft, affectionate kiss. I eagerly returned her kiss and held her close. She whispered in my ear; "Steve, if you invite me to stay my answer just might be yes."

We shared a long kiss, and I whispered; "You are most definitely invited."

We walked hand in hand down the dock toward Paradox. I helped her aboard, unlocked and opened the cabin door and reached for a light.

"Don't touch that light! Come in, close the door and put your hands out where I can see them."

In the dim light I could make out a short, muscular male figure with a handgun pointed at us.

"Well, well - I see you brought your girlfriend with you. Too bad."

"Sweetheart, sit your pretty ass down on that settee at the back of the cabin and keep your mouth shut if you know what's good for you."

As he spoke I realized my visitor was Alexander's yacht captain.

"Wilson, get this boat underway. We are headed to The Bahamas. I need to get out of the country and this is the best way. No funny business, remember when you go out to untie the lines that I have my gun on your girlfriend."

I was very nervous and it showed; "OK, give me a

few minutes to get the navigation systems turned on and the engine started."

My sweaty, shaking hands gripped the wheel as I got us underway, and we headed north up the Intracoastal toward the inlet to the ocean and The Bahamas.

"Can I ask how you got on my boat?"

"I saw where you put your spare key one day - I been here a lot and nobody pays much attention to crew. It was easy to follow another crew member through the security gate and open your cabin door last night. Been waiting for you all day and if you didn't show up soon I was going on my own tonight."

"Good you showed up, now you can't report the boat stolen. That could have been a problem."

"Alexander told me you were causing trouble when he called and told me to shred the documents in the safe, keep the cash and get lost."

He laughed and said; "This gives me the opportunity to get even with you when you go for a swim in about an hour. And thanks for bringing little sexpot along so I can have some fun before she takes a swim."

I felt sick; "Why do you want to kill us?"

"Why not? No witnesses and I don't trust Alexander not to turn on me to save his ass. Two more won't matter when I get out of the county and disappear."

Even when scared I guess I'm curious; "Two more, you mean Keith Jones and Donna don't you?"

"Don't get cute Wilson, but it doesn't make any difference, dead people like you don't talk."

"Stupid kid figured out the scam and got greedy. Stubborn little bastard wouldn't listen to me but it was an accident. Cover up worked like a charm."

"Silly girl got nervous when you recognized her. I was afraid she would crack. Alexander was pissed, but I had to keep her quiet."

"And Wilson, you were too stupid to take a hint - I thought the dead cat would stop your snooping around in our business."

We had turned toward the ocean and the wind from the East was creating a sizable wave pattern against the outgoing tide in the inlet. My natural instinct is to time the wave pattern and smoothly ride up each wave at a slight angle to soften the impact - but I was nervous and distracted. When I hit the third or fourth incoming wave head-on, it almost brought Paradox to a stop.

The captain and I both lost our balance. I crashed against the wheel and he grabbed the chart table as he stumbled forward to stay upright. In the confusion I heard a click from the back of the cabin and; "FBI, drop the gun!"

As I attempted to regain control of the boat, I glanced back and saw Amanda with her gun aimed at the captain. The captain didn't hesitate as he turned and fired his gun at Amanda.

I wasn't sure if I heard one or two shots as the glass window in the back of the cabin shattered. The captain slumped against the chart cabinet. He tried to recover and made a move to retrieve the gun he had just dropped on the cabin floor.

I was relieved when I heard Amanda say in a calm voice; "You touch that gun and I will shoot you in the balls next time. FBI - you are under arrest."

The captain shouted; "fuck you" as he slumped to the deck and leaned back against the chart cabinet. I could see blood spurting from his right shoulder.

"Steve, kick his gun to me and turn this vessel around."

"I'm trying. Amanda, are you all right?"

"Yes, I'm fine, don't worry about me."

I regained control, kicked the captain's gun back to Amanda and headed back into the Intracoastal.

Amanda told me to stop the boat after we returned to calm water. She kept her gun aimed at the captain while I tied his hands and feet together with plastic wire ties from my toolbox. Still shaking, I returned to the wheel and headed back to the marina.

Amanda then asked the location of my first aid kit and placed a bandage on the captain's wounded shoulder to stop the bleeding. He spit in her face to thank her.

Amanda called the local FBI office to report the incident and then called Mark to make certain he got her report first hand.

I pulled Paradox back into her slip and jumped on the dock to retie the dock lines. Once I got back onboard, I turned on the cabin lights.

"Amanda, you're covered in blood!"

"He was off balance - don't worry, he missed me. I just have a few cuts from the broken glass from that shattered window."

"Hold on, let me see if I can help."

Just then the FBI, local police and an ambulance

crew all converged on Paradox.

The next two hours were spent being interviewed, giving statements and filing reports. An FBI shooting requires lots of paperwork.

Finally, everybody departed and Amanda I were left sitting alone on the back deck of Paradox surrounded by yellow Do Not Cross tape.

I finally said; "What now, do you want a drink?

"Do you have Scotch?"

"Yes. Two Scotch on the rocks - on their way."

"Steve, we should both go back to the hotel until you can clean up this mess."

"I agree, I don't want to stay aboard Paradox tonight."

"I'm an excellent shot on the target range but that's the first time I ever fired at a person."

"Amanda, we were fortunate he didn't check if we were armed. Lucky he didn't take you seriously."

She replied; "Except to sneer and make crude gestures - what a creep."

"Steve, good work hitting that wave and knocking

him off balance."

"Amanda, that was an accident. I was too scared and nervous to steer properly. My hands were so sweaty I could barely control the boat. I'm thankful you were calm and ready with your gun."

"Let's go, I don't want to talk about it."

We had not checked out of the hotel when we went to dinner. Walking to Paradox was a spur-of-the-moment decision and our rooms were still available. We were both exhausted when we got to the hotel.

"Steve, it's been a rough night. Sorry, I no longer feel romantic. Maybe another time. Sleep well."

43

Saturday morning we skipped room service and walked to a cafe on Clematis that served breakfast.

"Steve, turn around - the news story on that TV is showing pictures of the marina and the sub-titles describe last night's events."

We realized we were watching a national news channel when the video switched back to the news anchor. The next segment showed my photo and the cover of my book!

I don't think either of us knew how to react and we looked at one another with bewildered expressions. A short while later both our cell phones started beeping with text messages.

I was getting multiple text messages in quick succession:

Ken Stewart; "We saw the news, are you OK? Give us a call!"

Darcy Levin; "What a mess, are you OK? Call me when you can."

Anne; "Frances just called. I don't carry a gun so we would both be dead. Glad you're OK."

# # #

Amanda had answered a call and walked a short distance down the sidewalk for some privacy. When she returned to the table, she said;

"That was my mother. I had to calm her down and explain the events last night were not nearly as sensational as described on TV. In fact, the way she described the story was confusing."

"The official statement we released reported a murder suspect was wounded in an exchange of gunfire with a female FBI agent on a boat belonging to you. The rest of the news story appears to be pure speculation."

"Oh, great! Steve, turn around again." Some reporter got passed the security gate and my photo from the book cover and a picture of Paradox with the yellow tape was now on the TV.

We noticed people were now beginning to stare. We quickly finished breakfast, paid the bill and departed. Amanda walked to the FBI office to review paperwork and make calls - she was still the agent in charge of the Alexander investigation.

I walked back to the hotel and called Ken; "Hi, I am OK but I would like to get out of Palm Beach. Would you mind if I came down to your guest house for a few days?"

2nd Week of December

Monday morning I took the train from Fort Lauderdale back to Palm Beach. The yellow tape had been removed, the reporters were gone and the events were now old news.

It seemed like everyone at the marina said "Hi" but most respected my privacy. I cleaned up the boat and made arrangements to replace the broken window and bloodstained carpet. I could find no other damage.

Wanda, my book editor, called on Tuesday: "Steve, have you been tracking book sales? Death Trap hit #3 on the mystery best seller list this morning. The publicity has been great for sales and several bookstores want to schedule signings. When can you get back to New York?"

"Wanda, that's amazing. No, I haven't been tracking sales. I am ready to get back to New York. See you tomorrow."

Wanda made the arrangements and the balance of

the week was media interviews and book signings. She stressed how important it was to take advantage of my "five minutes of fame" during the Holiday Season before I was "old news". Honestly, it was a great distraction.

I called Anne Sunday morning; we needed to talk. She didn't answer, so I left a voice mail.

About an hour later Anne sent a text message;

"Steve, I'm sorry but I don't want to talk. I enjoy being with you but the episode with the cat was unnerving. I knew it was a warning of some type."

"Your curiosity almost got me killed last year. You didn't tell me about being put in a closet at gunpoint or the trip to Nassau when that woman you went to meet was murdered. If I had been with you in Palm Beach, we would both be dead. I can't be part of such a dangerous relationship. Please try to stay safe."

44

3rd Week of December

Mark asked me to meet him in his office Monday morning to review the Alexander case. I wasn't surprised Amanda was also at the meeting.

Mark started; "Steve, we have located Alexander in London and are making arrangements to request extradition. He has retained an attorney and is aware of the events in Palm Beach. He denies any knowledge about the deaths of Keith Jones or Donna Hawkins. His attorney said if any crime was committed it was due to the captain going rogue."

"The captain was right that night on your boat when he said Alexander would turn on him. As insurance, he didn't shred all the documents in the boat's safe. He had dozens of incriminating documents and over a million dollars in cash from the safe in his travel bag."

"We don't have enough evidence at this time to charge Alexander or his captain for murder."

"The captain's firing his gun at Amanda, an FBI Special Agent, is currently his downfall. The only evidence thus far that connects him directly to the deaths of Keith and Donna are his statements to you and Amanda on your boat."

"The statements we have from Alexander's accountant and the bank's account officer in Boston are more than enough to convict Alexander of fraud."

"I wanted to keep you up-to-date and thank you for your help. Once again your curiosity uncovered a significant fraud. Well done."

"Finally, I think Amanda wants to take you to dinner tonight - you have earned a special meal and you guys can talk tonight."

#   #   #

As Amanda and I walked out, I suggested a quiet neighborhood restaurant and made arrangements to meet her at eight o'clock. I was early as usual and Amanda walked in the door promptly at eight.

Amanda waited to talk until after we were seated and ordered a glass of wine;

"Steve, my actions last week weren't just spur-of-the-moment. The more time we spend together the more I like being with you. It scares me."

I smiled; "Amanda, I feel the same way and it scares me too. It's like you said, any personal relationship could get very complicated. We have both just started new careers that overlap and they could also go in very different directions."

"Steve, you kissed me on the dock that night and invited me to stay - did you mean it?"

I caressed her hand, looked her in the eye and replied; "Yes, I definitely wanted you to stay."

"Steve, that's good because I want you to know I am very open with Mark. After the fact, I told him I planned to stay with you on your boat that night. The captain just interrupted our plans."

"What did Mark say?"

"He suggested we have dinner and work out what's best for us. He only asks that I let him know if, at any time, our relationship might compromise an investigation."

"Steve, I have had time to think this past week and I want to take it slow and see what happens. I am not going to accept an invitation to go to your apartment tonight."

She added; "I don't know what your plans are for Christmas next week but I will be with my family in Maine. I have a few vacation days and don't have plans for New Year's Eve. I would love to be with you if that works for you."

I raised her hand to my lips; "Amanda, that would be wonderful. I would love to start the New Year with you. Where would you like to meet?"

"New York."

Epilogue

Sad to say I had given no thought to plans for Christmas. In prior years, I had always joined a group of friends from the city to celebrate. At the last minute, I joined them again. It was a nice break to share the holiday with old friends and to join them for parties in their apartments and at various gathering places around the city.

I had lunch with Mark during the holiday week and we discussed my plans for the next several months. I told him; "Based on the response to Death Trap, my editor wants me to make time to write another book. I enjoy writing and I told her I would make that my priority in the new year."

"Like last time, I will base it on my notes about recent events and, once again, I will change all the names and write the story as fiction."

Mark asked; "Do you have a title?"

"Yes, I think so. This whole episode started when Keith deceived his wife and was discovered dead in the turquoise waters of Thunderball Grotto. We plan to call it Turquoise Deception."

Mark asked; "What about your consulting practice?"

"I plan to restrict my consulting activity to existing clients. I don't plan to accept new clients until the book is published."

Mark interrupted; "Steve, I want to make certain you continue your consulting relationship with the FBI. Your services have been invaluable."

I assured him I would and he responded; "Good, because I have a situation developing in DC that might require your services."

#   #   #

Amanda and I made plans to meet in New York to celebrate the New Year. She made it clear she wanted to spend several days touring the city, visiting museums, going to the theater and sampling a wide variety of restaurants.

Her final comment was:

"I will let you know where I plan to stay the day I arrive."

TURQUOISE DECEPTION

Dedication

Molly, Linda & Martha

For your encouragement and patience

Acknowledgements

Our visits by boat to The Bahamas and along the east coast from Florida to Maine have provided extensive information and insight about the locations described in Turquoise Deception.
I am very grateful to the following:

Boothbay Harbor Marina
Brooklin Boat Yard
Exuma Land & Sea Park
Front Street Shipyard
Highbourne Cay
Palm Harbor Marina
Staniel Cay Yacht Club

Photos

Molly Potter Thayer
Paul Harding
Palm Harbor Marina

About the Author

Charles Thayer is the author of Death Trap, A Murder Mystery, and numerous business books and articles. Turquoise Deception is book two of the Paradox Murder Mysteries.

Charles and his wife, Molly, and their dog, Scupper, enjoy cruising in The Bahamas and along the east coast from Florida to Maine aboard their Duffy 37, a custom Maine built lobster boat.

Charles enjoyed a fifty-year career in the banking industry having served as an executive officer and as a board member of several banking institutions. His Paradox mystery series blend his experience as a financial executive with his love of cruising.

Additional information is available at:

www.Paradox-Research.com

Paradox09A@Gmail.com

Paradox Murder Mystery

Book One: Death Trap

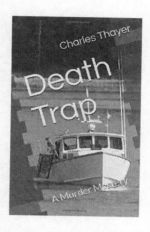

Learn how the story begins as Steve Wilson travels to Maine to unwind, enjoy the coastal scenery and write a murder mystery novel.

Steve's years of unraveling financial mysteries from the safety of his bank office did not prepare him for the dangers he faced in Maine when his curiosity about a dead lobsterman, a deserted lobster boat and three missing photos almost got him killed.

Death Trap is Steve's description of his unexpected adventure in Maine.

Books by Charles J Thayer

Fiction

2018   *Death Trap, A Murder Mystery*

Non-Fiction

2017   *Bank Director Survival Guide*
           Chartwell Publications

2016   *Credit Check*
           Giving Credit Where Credit Is Due

2010   *It Is What It Is*
           Saving American West Bank

1986   *The Bank Director's Handbook;*
           Auburn House: 2nd Edition
           Chapter: Asset/Liability Management

1983   *Bankers Desk Reference*
           Warren, Gorham & Lamont
           Chapter: Financial Futures Market

1981   *The Bank Director's Handbook;*
           Auburn House: 1st Edition
           Chapter: Asset/Liability Management

Made in the USA
Lexington, KY
29 April 2019